Owlhoot Trail

Owlhoot Trail

CLIFF FARRELL

Sagebrush
Large Print Westerns

Library of Congress Cataloging in Publication Data

Farrell, Cliff.
   Owlhoot trail / Cliff Farrell.
     p.   cm.
   ISBN 1-57490-056-0 (hc : alk. paper)
   1. Large type books. I. Title.
[PS3556.A766O94   1997]
813'.54--dc20   96-53967
                                                    CIP

Cataloguing in Publication Data is available from
the British Library and the National Library of Australia.

Sagebrush Large Print Westerns are published in the United States
and Canada by Thomas T. Beeler, Publisher, Box 659, Post Office
Hampton Falls, New Hampshire 03844-0659. ISBN 1-57490-056-0

Published in the United Kingdom, Eire, and the Republic of South
Africa by Isis Publishing Ltd, 7 Centremead, Osney Mead, Oxford
OX2 0ES England. ISBN 0-7531-5524-9

Published in Australia and New Zealand by Australian Large Print
Audio & Video Pty Ltd, 17 Mohr Street, Tullamarine, Victoria, 3043,
Australia. ISBN 1-86340-687-5

Manufactured in the United States of America

CHAPTER 1

GONE TOMORROW WAS A COMMUNITY THAT HAD BEEN born only days ago, and soon it would be no more. In the near past it had been an untamed, empty stretch of prairie, untouched, unplowed, stretching vacantly beneath the April sky along the northern border of what cowboys and trail drivers called The Nations and what newcomers called Oklahoma Territory.

Now Gone Tomorrow was a disturbed human anthill—a ragtag collection of boomers and sooners, of thieves and farmers, of men hungry for free land, and of sharpers who had flocked here in search of prey. Gone Tomorrow was miles in length and as thin as a snake. It had no religion, no future, and little law. Its life was to be short, but on this day in April it was a sight to see.

Vance Barret gazed at these sights as he rode into what was the biggest of Gone Tomorrow's several hearts. He rode a fine roan saddlehorse and led a handsome, slim-barreled chestnut equipped with only a headstall and a surcingle. He followed a rambling semblance of a street along which was clotted a straggle of dancehalls, gambling houses, saloons, brothels and stores—all under canvas, all poised to fold their wings and fly south when the race for land came. Here was the blare and hurrah of an exploding new country. Here was music and revelry. Painted women in plumed hats rubbed elbows with the sedate wives of sodbusters who carried market baskets on their arms. Swaggering, tough men crowded tenderfeet off the dirt paths.

A hoarse-voiced evangelist exhorted a group of cynical listeners to repent their sins. A mustachioed medicine-

1

show professor in a stovepipe hat and rusty frock coat vied with leather-lunged barkers at the dancehalls, proclaiming the cure-all virtues of his bottled offerings. He strutted about on the platform attached to a wagon from which the gilt was fading. On the same platform, a girl in spangled costume occasionally did a few dance steps, slapping a tambourine, and took in the dollars of the gullible who believed in the professor's promises.

Down the street, troubleshooters ejected a drunken man from a gambling house, sending him tumbling headlong into the dust. The victim was a cowboy, young and befuddled. He arose to his feet, a six-shooter in his hand. He was blasted to death by the pistols of the two gunmen before he could fire.

The shooting gave pause to the revelry. The tumult of voices stilled. Wagon teams were dragged to a halt. The grinding voices of the barkers, of the evangelist and of the medicine-show faker tapered off. Only the beat of drums in distant houses of pleasure continued faintly.

The evangelist moved in and started to intone a prayer over the victim. He was pushed aside by a man on whose vest was pinned the star of a federal marshal. The officer asked perfunctory questions of the killers and eyewitnesses and told them to be available for an inquest that would be held as soon as a jury could be impaneled. He commandeered a wagon into which the body was placed, and rode away on the seat with the driver.

The incident was over. The killers disappeared into the dancehall to resume their duties. The crosscurrents of vehicular and saddle movement set in once more. The barkers and the medicine-show professor resumed their spiels. But the face of the girl on the platform was ghastly pale. She turned suddenly and vanished into the shelter of the gilded wagon.

2

Vance rode to the hitchrail of one of the gambling houses and dismounted. The chestnut horse commanded immediate attention. It had a striking white blaze on its forehead, and both front legs were white to the knees. Men came to gaze, some admiringly, some with envy, some with calculation.

"That blazeface is a mighty purty hawss, mister," one remarked. "He's got a lot o' Kaintuck blood, I'd say. An' what else?"

"Some mustang, maybe," Vance said. "Some curly wolf, some cutting horse, something of most everything good. You're right about the Kentucky. He's half thoroughbred. His name is Rajah, sired by Emperor II."

Vance produced a whiskbroom from a saddle pocket and began flicking dust from his apparel. He wore tailored saddle garb and bench-made boots. His vest was of watered silk over a fine linen shirt that had a ruffle down the front.

"Kin he run?" the man asked.

Vance laughed. "Can an eagle fly? Can the wind blow?"

"You aimin' on runnin' him here?"

"Hadn't given it a thought," Vance said. "Could be, if there's competition to make it worthwhile."

"There's a track laid out there yonder on the flats," the man said. He was long and lean. He wore a beaded vest and a calico shirt that was stuffed into striped cowboy breeches. His boots had runover heels. His voice was as reedy as his length. "They race every afternoon. An' do some bettin'."

"I might look into it," Vance said.

"You've still got plenty of time," the man informed him. "Racin' starts at two o'clock."

"Don't rush me, friend," Vance said. "I haven't had time to get the saddleburs off me. I'm on my way from Dodge to Fort Smith, and passed by to watch the run. I

3

didn't say I was going to risk Rajah in a prairie-dog race, did I? I'm figuring on better things."

"Ain't you goin' to make the run?" asked the beanpole.

Vance laughed again. "Do I look like a man who'd spend his time grubbing out bunch grass so I could raise rutabagas? I only came down to watch. It ought to be quite a sight."

He produced a coin from a vest pocket and tossed it. The reedy man caught it and uttered a whistle of surprise. "A half eagle!" he exclaimed. "Now, what—?"

"That's to see that my roan, who answers to the name of Pawnee, and the blazeface, are watered, and enjoy a little grain and hay. What's your name, tall man?"

"I'm Jim Leatherwood," the man said. "Now, wait a minute, mister. Maybe I don't cotton to bein' responsible for—"

"Make mighty sure that nothing happens to either of them, Leatherwood, if that's really your name," Vance said. He casually loosened his coat so that Leatherwood and other onlookers had a glimpse of the gun he carried in a holster. It was a .44 Colt with a polished cedar handle.

Leatherwood's Adam's apple gyrated. "I'll do my best," he said. "All I ask is that you don't stay too long, mister."

Vance placed the reins of the roan and the chestnut's lead rope in Leatherwood's hands. "Just tell me where you will take care of them and where I can find you when I want them, and there'll be the other half of that eagle in it if you earn it. My name is Barret, Vance Barret."

Leatherwood walked at his side, leading the horses as they moved away from the group. "I'll take back that

4

goldpiece now," Vance murmured. "I need one to rub against the other."

"I figgered you was overdoin' it a little, Vance, slingin' five-dollar pieces around like they was pennies." Leatherwood sighed as he slipped the goldpiece back into Vance's hand. "Are you that near bottom? You hit a bad run somewhere?"

"At Dodge while I was waiting for your letter," Vance said. "Cards ran against me for three straight nights. I couldn't even improve openers in jackpots."

"You should have shortcarded 'em, dang it."

"It wasn't that kind of play," Vance said. "Everybody was tough but playing on the level. Good clean poker. It wouldn't have been decent."

Leatherwood sighed again. "If you ain't the one. What's decency got to do with it when the patches on the seat of my pants are getting thin? Lucky you didn't lose Rajah in your honest game. When will you ever admit that it's dog eat dog in this world, an' the devil take them that can't spot a cold deck? Where did you leave Iggy and Rip Van Winkle?"

"Camped in the brush alongside that creek you can see out in the flats, but about an hour's ride upstream. Just follow the creek until you come on an open stand of post oak. Don't pack any firewater. I want Iggy kept sober. Have you lined up anything?"

"No linin' up needed. This here place is ripe for the pickin'. Every tinhorn an' cutthroat from hell to Texas is here."

"Any fast horses?"

"Two or three. The rest air cowhorses and Injun ponies. In-an'-outers. One day they run, the next time they quit. They mostly quit when a good horse looks 'em in the eye."

5

"Any that can run with Rajah?"

"There's one that might give him a race. A black mare they call Lightnin' Flash. I got a hunch I seen that mare run at Denver under another name. Likely she was stolen. She's fast, but Rajah should take her."

"Who stole her?"

"Well, the hombres what claim to own her go by the names of George an' Henry Jones here in G.T. They stole them names, too. Their real hind names are Nello."

Vance gave Leatherwood a surprised look. "Not *the* Nellos?"

"None other," Leatherwood said. "Two of 'em was in the bunch that was lookin' you an' the runner over back there. Maybe you noticed 'em. Both has got that cold-jawed, milky-eyed expression. Art Nello's got a purple knife scar on his cheek. Lige is the ugly one with the flattened nose an' bowed laigs. They try to dress like boomers. The other one is here too—Chick Nello. He's the smart one, with brains. Maybe you didn't savvy them, but they knowed who you was the minute you mentioned your name."

"You're sure?"

Leatherwood scorned to answer that. "What I mean," Vance said apologetically, "is to wonder why they haven't been picked up. Everybody knows the Nello bunch stuck up that Santa Fe express west of Dodge not long ago and got away with a big wad of money. Why?"

"That's a good question," Leatherwood said.

"There's at least one federal marshal here," Vance said. "He ought to know who they are."

"Along with some Wells Fargo agents."

"I can see you're busting with news," Vance said. "Maybe it better wait. We're doing too much talking for new acquaintances."

6

A large shadow moved between them. A heavy forefinger tapped Vance aggressively on the chest. The forefinger belonged to the bulky federal marshal. At this close range Vance saw that the officer had weathered, prune-wrinkled features.

"I got enough misery tryin' to keep law and order here without you showing up, Barret," the marshal said. "I'm Ben Wheat, and I enforce the law in G.T. I'm just warning you that I'll throw you into the stockade along with the other tinhorns and sooners the first wrong move you make. We want no sleeve aces nor sleight-of-hand at the poker tables in this camp. Above all, no shooting."

Vance looked down coldly at the aggressive forefinger. In his hand the six-shooter had appeared. He cocked back the hammer, placed the muzzle against the marshal's finger. "In a second or two they'll be calling you Four-fingered Ben, Marshal," he said.

The finger was hastily removed from his chest. Ben Wheat backed off a pace. He was careful not to make any hasty motion that might be mistaken as an attempt to go for his own armament. "I'm warnin' you—," he began.

"So I'm warned," Vance said. He holstered his weapon, pushed past the marshal and walked away. Leatherwood joined him.

The encounter had taken place in front of the platform of the medicine show. The painted girl in the spangled dress had returned to the platform, and had been listening. Vance removed his hat, swept it low in a flourishing bow. "The top of the morning to you, miss."

"To you," she said, "the name is Princess Delilah."

"A fine name," Vance said. "I hope you and the professor sell a hundred bottles of snake oil today."

7

He expected her to blast him with indignation. Instead, she only smiled with disarming sweetness. "Snake oil is better than dealing second card or palming aces for the suckers. I heard the marshal warn you against crooked dealing or starting trouble here in G.T., Mr. Barret. How soon are you leaving?"

"I haven't decided," Vance said. "All I know is that a female with a sharp tongue is an abomination unto the Lord, and to me. That may decide me that this is no place for me. I will offer up a prayer that you mend your ways."

She placed her hands on her hips and laughed jeeringly at him. "Go on your way, Mr. Barret," she said. "You are driving paying customers away. As for praying, do not forget to put in a word for yourself."

"I'll keep that in mind," Vance said.

"I doubt if you know any of the words," she replied.

Vance gave her another flourishing bow, and he and Leatherwood moved on. The painted banner above the platform informed one and all that the medicine show was the possession of one Professor Schyler Fortune, and that the famed oracle and prophetess Princess Delilah would offer palm readings and predictions of the future.

"I'd say, from her accent, that Princess Delilah was born somewhere west of the Mississippi, maybe in Texas, and that she was christened something like Sadie Simple," Vance said.

"New Mexico, not Texas," Leatherwood said. "And Simple her name is not. Nor simple is she. You'd be surprised."

"You evidently are a fountain of information today and will burst unless you are allowed to spout," Vance said. "First there were the Jones brothers who are really the Nello brothers. Now you seem to know about the secret

8

lives of Professor Schyler and Princess Delilah. But first questions first. Why haven't the Nellos been arrested by our heavy-fingered friend Mr. Wheat, or by the express agents that you say are infesting this camp?"

"Arrested? For what?"

"For what? For sticking up that Santa Fe flyer. What else?"

"Who says they did?"

Vance eyed him. "Everybody says they did."

"The Nellos have already been jugged three or four times by ambitious sheriffs an' such," Leatherwood said. "An' turned loose. You just can't put people in jail because everybody only *thinks* they're guilty. You know that—or ought to. You've been in the same boat a few times, bein' as your name is Barret. But under the law, you got to have evidence. Or witnesses. The fellers what stuck up that train an' blew the Wells Fargo safe was all masked in slickers an' gunny sacks. Nobody could really testify as to what they looked like."

"Keep talking," Vance said. "I can see that you haven't got to the point yet."

"Them masked fellers got away with around eighty thousand dollars in good, cashable gold notes. Said gold notes still seem to be missin'. Nobody seems to want to jail nobody, I reckon, 'til that money turns up an' gets back into the hands of its owners, namely, Wells Fargo and Company."

Vance peered closely at his angular companion. "Continue," he said.

"How do you know I ain't said enough?"

"How do you know I won't twist it out of that pipestem neck of yours?"

"Shucks, your sweetness would make me choke all up," Leatherwood said. "No, don't hit me. I won't waste

9

no more of my jokes on you. It looks to me like there are some folks here in G.T. what seem to think that dinero is cached somewhere around here."

"You mean down in The Nations?"

"I'd say that'd be a mighty good guess."

"So the Nello brothers hid it down there and are going in on the run to lift the cache?"

"I reckon that if they knowed where it was cached they'd have lifted it long ago an' been long gone to Mexico. They know that country down there. They've hid out there more than once. They punched cattle as young squirts before they turned to holdin' up trains an' such. They could have soonered in weeks ago before the cal'vry plugged up the loopholes."

"Quit circling the tree, and show me the possum," Vance said. "What are you trying to back into?"

"That train was held up by *five* men, accordin' to the passengers. There happens to be only three Nello brothers. You'll see two of 'em, if you want to look back. They're still standing back there, watchin' you an' the blazeface. I'll point out the other one, Chick, if he happens along. He's not only the smartest, but he's bad medicine from the chunk. A real killer. He'd murder his own father if it suited him. Never underestimate Chick Nello. He goes by the name of Bill Sands around here."

"Underestimate him? I don't even know him—or want to." "The other two that was in on the stickup wasn't Nellos. They're the ones who got away with the money."

"How's that again?"

"One was a wild young greenhorn who'd never been in on a thing like that before. The Nellos let him hold the horses, includin' the pack animals on which the money was put after the express safe had been blown.

10

Him an' the other fellow lit out with the livestock an' the money, leavin' the Nellos afoot. The Nellos smoked them up some, but it was dark an' rainin' hard, an' they got away."

"Very interesting," Vance said. "But our business is trying to keep the wolf from the door. To do this, I hope to play a little successful poker and win a horse race or two."

"There's a reward of five thousand dollars, dead or alive, put up by the Santa Fe Railway, for any of the gang that pulled the holdup. The engineer an' the Wells Fargo messenger were killed by one of the gang. Shot in cold blood. It was Chick, of course. He's the kind for that sort of thing. Then there's eighty thousand dollars that's waitin' somewhere to be picked up by the finder."

"Nice weather we're having," Vance said.

Leatherwood sighed again. "Get behind me, Satan," he said. "You're right, but it's interestin' to sit on the sidelines. The Nellos ain't the only ones that are hangin' around G.T. on account of that eighty thousand. It happens there are other folks here that are more than a little bit interested in that express money."

"Maybe I don't want to know."

"What if I told you that these other folks might just happen to be a slick-talkin' old buzzard what wears a stovepipe hat an' tries to sell sugar pap for a dollar a bottle, along with a gal who claims to be a fortuneteller?"

"The medicine-show faker and the Princess Delilah? Are you sober, Jim?"

"It happens that the professor was named plain Henry Judson when I knew him ten years or so ago down in Santa Fe, where I was workin' as bouncer at a honkytonk. He was a preacher in them days."

11

"A *preacher?* That old thimble-rigger?"

"He was a widower with some kids to feed, as I remember it. A couple of scrawny young girls an' a boy about seven or eight. One of the two what doubledecked the Nellos that night happened to be named Judson. Frank Judson. He was only about eighteen, accordin' to my information."

Leatherwood let that sink in. Vance finally spoke. "After all, the professor and the girl *could* only be after a homestead on the run."

"Sure. One with eighty thousand dollars buried in it."

"That holdup was pulled a couple of months ago," Vance argued. "By this time, this Frank Judson and his pal likely are in Mexico, or maybe South America, living it up."

"This same information tells me they're both dead."

"Dead?"

"Remember me sayin' that the Nellos smoked 'em up that night when they cleared out with the horses an' the money? Well, the Nellos didn't miss. Frank Judson's pal was a reckless young hellion, like himself, named Clem Barker. He was hit by slugs an' died the next day at the ranch of a relative where Frank Judson brought him. Judson was wounded pretty bad, but rode off, sayin' he knew where he would get help. The professor was operatin' his medicine show in Dodge at that time. Young Judson's never been seen since. My information tells me that he died an' that his folks buried him somewhere around Dodge a day or two after the stickup."

"The money?"

"It's my guess that somebody hid it down in The Nations, to wait until the opening so that it could be picked up under cover of the confusion. An' that

12

somebody is Professor Schyler Fortune, otherwise Henry Judson."

"I've heard all I want to hear," Vance said. "Forget about the money. Forget about the Judsons and the Nellos. Let the Nellos and the Judsons squabble over it. Over the ghosts that go with it. It's got a life term in prison tied to it. Two men were murdered. I can see a hangrope in the background. We've got other fish to fry. Small fish, but not tainted with blood. And we've also been palavering here in public too long. Somebody might begin to suspect we're not the strangers we pretend to be."

A column of cavalrymen rode by, giving them excuse for additional conversation as they waited for the dust to clear. The troopers, sabers swaying in saddleboots, boredom in their weather-darkened faces, were escorting half a dozen army wagons loaded with apathetic civilian prisoners. These were sooners who had been caught south of the deadline. They were bound for the stockade where they would be held for trial, or at least until too late to take part in the initial land rush. They were jeered and taunted by boomers along the way. Stones and clods were hurled at the wagons. The troopers ducked clear, laughing, and made no attempt to interfere.

Vance listened to sounds from the biggest of the canvas-roofed gambling houses, named the Buffalo Palace, which stood nearby. "Straight games?" he asked.

"Are you loco? Straight—in this place? Every roulette wheel is fixed with magnets. A house man sets at the high-play poker tables with spring clips in his sleeves an' a slide drawer at his knees holdin' cold decks. It's run by Johnny Briscoe."

"Enough said," Vance remarked. "So Johnny's here, all the way from Denver to take the suckers. How much money have you got on you? I need a little more leeway than ten dollars and some chicken feed if I'm going to play poker."

Leatherwood sighed some more. He drew a wad of crumpled bills from a pocket, pretending that he was sampling a plug of tobacco, and handed it quickly over to Vance. "There's more'n a hundred dollars in it," he lamented.

"A *hundred?* Who did you rob?"

"You know I'm through with that sort o' thing," Leatherwood said, injured. "I been playin' a leetle pool here an' there. Fer money. An' I won more'n fifty yesterday in a turkey shoot."

"Did they know who they were up against?"

Leatherwood grinned. "Seems like they found out. I'm barred from the shoots from now on. An' I can't find anybody that wants to play pool ag'in me any more."

During one phase of a very checkered career, Jim Leatherwood had traveled—under another name—with the Buffalo Bill Wild West Show, giving demonstrations of marksmanship with rifles and pistols in the circus rings. He had been ballyhooed as the greatest crackshot in the world, a claim that was not far from the truth. At other, darker times, he had traveled with the longriders—outlaws. He knew the twisted maze of the owlhoot trails, knew its followers. He was trusted by men who still rode outside the law, and had sources of information that would have been beyond price to any sheriff or marshal.

"Where will I find you?" Vance asked.

Leatherwood pointed. "There's a thief what runs a livery feed yard up the line aways. You can't miss it. It's about the only place you can buy a bait of grain—if

14

you've got the price. I'll see to it that Rajah an' Pawnee get clean water an' some hay. My own horse is staked out at the camp of a friend of mine I can trust. This place is full of horse thieves."

"Go easy on both the water and grain, as far as Rajah is concerned," Vance said.

"You aim on runnin' him today? So soon?"

"Time's short, and he's ready. Iggy has worked him every day on the prairie on the way from Dodge. Can we find a spot for him at the track this afternoon?"

"I reckon. They hold ten, maybe a dozen sprints every afternoon, mainly for crowbait stock, with ten- or twenty-dollar purses. The best race is the last one, with sometimes as high as a hundred to the winner. It costs twenty to enter the feature race."

"I'll play a little poker for an hour or so, and maybe I can run up a stake," Vance said. "I'll meet you at this feed yard. I'll take Rajah and find a camp down by the creek. You can ride upstream and locate Iggy. Send him in with the wagon and Rip Van Winkle."

"How is that old cuss, Rip?" Leatherwood asked.

"Eating hearty as usual, sleeping it off as usual, loafing as usual."

"I sort of like that danged mulehead," Leatherwood said. "Independent. That's what he is. Takes life easy. Someday he's goin' to git sassy an' show Rajah how a horse can really run fast."

"That will indeed be the day," Vance said. "I've invested a lot of hay in that animal, and would like some return. No more talk now. We've done too much of it already."

Leatherwood walked away, leading the two horses. Vance gazed toward the medicine-show wagon. "Professor Schyler Fortune" had managed to attract

15

additional listeners. Vance decided the real attraction was "Princess Delilah." She was young and shapely. In spite of the powder and paint, she was obviously good-looking. She had curly, dark hair and large dark eyes. She was drawing aside a curtain which revealed the entrance to a small cubby adorned with the signs of the Zodiac, a large drawing of the human palm, and other typical emblems of the fortuneteller's lair. A crystal ball stood on a table.

The professor was bellowing through a megaphone: "And now, ladies and gentlemen, I call your attention to Princess Delilah, descendant of a royal Egyptian line, who is gifted with a talent no other human in the world possesses—the power to divine the future. Which of you has the bravery—the fortitude—to enter the mystic domain of the princess and learn your fate? Which of you, I say?"

The spiel droned on. "Princess Delilah" did not seem to be listening. She was gazing in Vance's direction. At first, Vance flattered himself by believing he was the object of her interest. Then he realized that her eyes were not on him, but on something beyond him. Her gaze was following Leatherwood and the horses he was leading away.

CHAPTER 2

SOMEWHAT CHAGRINED, VANCE TURNED AND ENTERED the Buffalo Palace. Even at this prenoon hour the place was busy. Its canvas top was hazed with tobacco smoke. A band labored at banjos, horns and drums, on a platform set on sawhorses at the rear. A long bar built of planks ran nearly the length of the tent to the right. Gambling layouts crowded the remainder of the space

16

around a tiny dance floor, covered with sawdust, which was not being used at this hour.

Vance moved to the bar and inspected prices that were chalked on a board on the back bar:

Beer	$ .50
Cold Beer	$1.00
Water	$ .25
Cold Water	$ .50
Whisky	$ .75
Gin	$ .50
Kentucky W.	$1.00
Tomcat G.	$ .50

"Cold beer," Vance said to a beefy barkeeper who moved indolently to face him.

The beer came from a spigot, thick with foam in a heavy-bottomed mug. It was far from being cold.

Vance tossed a silver dollar on the bar. The barkeeper scorned it. "That'll be two dollars, mister," he said.

Vance looked up at the price list. The figure for cold beer had magically changed. It was now quoted at two dollars. He saw that all prices were on sliding panels that could be manipulated, evidently, by the barkeepers. Patrons around him were snickering, and waiting with anticipation.

Vance leaned across the bar and located the wired controls. He pulled one, by guess, and guessed right. On the price board the slide moved, and the one-dollar figure was restored.

"In addition, it wasn't cold," Vance said. "Next time, make sure it *is* cold."

The barkeeper also leaned over the bar and started to swing a beefy fist. The fist paused, poised, for the man found himself looking into the bore of Vance's six-shooter.

"Were you going to say something?" Vance asked.

The man subsided. With a sickly grin, he picked up the coin, tossed it in the cash drawer. "A wise guy," he said half-admiringly. "With a nod of my head I could bring in some fellers who're paid to take care of people like you."

"Nod away," Vance said.

"You ain't lookin' for a farm, I take it," the barkeeper said. "You ain't got the looks."

"You could be right," Vance said.

The barkeeper moved away. Vance holstered his gun and leaned against the bar while he appraised the room. Four poker tables were in operation. A ball skittered around a roulette wheel. A birdcage revolved, the dice bouncing against the bars. Other dice banged on the crap tables.

Play was loud and noisy at the majority of the games where stakes were small, with the players obviously only out to pass the time without much risk. No house man was involved in these games.

One of the poker tables was separated from the common play by a roped enclosure from which spectators were barred. A sign hung on the tent wall above this table announcing that this was an open game, the rules to be set by the house. A smaller blackboard beneath the painted sign stated that, at present, the limit of a wager was ten dollars, with the raises limited at three. The game was draw poker, three-card limit.

Five men were playing. Two were quietly, almost somberly dressed, and might be taken for drummers or clerks. The way they handled the cards told the truth. They lived by their wits.

A third man wore a black eyeshade and a black vest, proclaiming that he played for the house. There was something vaguely familiar about the fourth player. He was a hard-jawed, big man who looked to be about forty. Sandy sideburns framed milky eyes beneath a tall-crowned range hat. There was an aggressive set to his thin lips. Vance suddenly remembered the two brothers Leatherwood had mentioned, recalled their eyes. The family resemblance was plain. This must be Chick Nello, the third member of the outlaw brotherhood.

Vance sipped the tepid beer as he sized up the other player. This one was well-dressed, cagey and in his fifties. He had a gray mustache, and a gold watch chain was draped across his front. Vance judged that he was not only an experienced player, but was a businessman who had plenty of money to overcome opposition. He evidently was a poker hobbyist who liked to match his skill against professionals—a dangerous opponent, for he played by whim, and his moves could not be anticipated. He was also vain and proud, the kind who would try to bluff out an inferior hand by sheer weight of money.

Vance continued to appraise the players. He had learned that judging the nature of opponents was the key to success at poker. The two frayed-cuff gamblers he discounted. They were betting warily, obviously on limited funds like himself, careful to hoard their resources by dropping out of hopeless pots early. They faced a bleak task against the house man and the gray-mustached opponent.

While the play Vance watched was apparently on the level, he was certain that the formation of the table lent itself to concealed spring clips and slide drawers that held cards or cold decks which could be produced instantly into under-the-table hands. In addition, the house man sat facing the tent wall, with his opponents backed by what was apparently only blank canvas, wrinkled and weather-stained—a perfect setup for slits and peepholes.

19

However, Vance decided that the game was being played without trickery—for the moment, at least. No doubt, the stakes were not worth risking deception that might be discovered. The play was casual, with little bludgeoning. It differed from the games at other tables only because silver dollars and greenbacks were being used to buy chips instead of the five-for-a-quarter price that was the general rule. The play was quiet and more serious than the noisy card-thumping and laughter at the minor games.

Vance carefully studied the thin-eyed big man—Chick Nello. He was a pusher, a bully who tried to frighten his opposition by limit bets on short-card draws. It was, Vance surmised, Chick Nello's way of life. He knew men of Nello's kind—knew them too well. That was why Ben Wheat had warned him that he was unwelcome in Gone Tomorrow, and why Leatherwood had told him that Lige and Art Nello had recognized his name when he had given it. He was one of the outlaw Barrets—the last of them. He was the son of Jubal Barret, who, along with two of Vance's brothers, had robbed trains, banks and stagecoaches from Missouri to California. In their day they had been known as the Wild Barret Bunch.

The Barret Bunch rode no more. Jubal Barret was dead, along with two of his sons. They had all gone out with their boots on, asking no quarter or favors, offering no surrender, dying as they had lived—undisciplined, untamed.

It was common belief that Vance, youngest of the brood, had ridden with his kinsmen. He had been arrested many times by glory-hunting sheriffs and marshals, but there had never been any legal evidence on which to convict him. The only result was that it had generated in him a vast contempt for humanity in general, and a

20

cynical determination to take advantage of the gullibility and weaknesses of any who tried to prey on him.

He had learned to short-card or second-card a poker deal with velvet speed and adroitness, and he had become expert in beating crooked gamblers at their own game. He could draw the cedar-handled .44 as fast as any man he had ever seen in action. It was said that he had killed at least half a dozen men. Once an opponent became aware he was dealing with Vance Barret, the man's desire to settle an issue with pistols usually evaporated.

Vance had won thousands of dollars at single sittings at poker. He had lost equally large sums at other sessions. Win or lose, no man had ever seen a change of expression in his eyes or lean face. When he chose, no one could read any hint of the emotions that played within him—or realize how fierce were those fires at times. Only two men were close enough to him to share his secrets. Jim Leatherwood was one. Leatherwood was past fifty, and had ridden with Jubal Barret in the old, wild days. He now rode with Vance.

The other was Ignacio Guadalupe Espinosa, whose father had been one of the Barret longriders. Iggy was a slim, handsome, free spirit of Vance's age and viewpoint. He wore the tallest heels he could endure on his boots in an attempt to match Vance's and Leatherwood's six feet of height. His weight, which he attempted to keep secret, was one hundred and sixteen pounds, but he could handle the roughest horses, and he was the most graceful figure in a saddle that Vance had ever seen.

Vance tried to continue his study of the poker players, but a part of his mind kept turning to the surprising information Leatherwood had passed along. He had known better than to ask the source of such information, but knowing the tall man, he was certain it was accurate.

21

Eighty thousand dollars. In spite of himself, that figure kept running temptingly through his mind. He wondered if the medicine-show professor and Princess Delilah were aware of the real identity of the Nellos, and the reason for their presence in Gone Tomorrow.

Leatherwood had mentioned that the railroad had put up five thousand dollars reward for information that might lead to arrest of the guilty. It was common knowledge that the express company had a standing offer of 10 percent of all money recovered from such information. That would amount to another eight thousand dollars. The two bounties would add up to quite a stake for hand-to-mouth drifters like himself and his companions.

Angered at himself for letting his mind carry down that path, he tried to turn his attention completely to the poker game. He had made a pledge to himself in the past—one that he had kept in spite of great temptation at times. At least, until now.

He concentrated on the game, trying to forget such names as Judson and Nello. His stake was small, but to him it was vitally important. He debated whether he should even risk that meager amount at this time. For him and Iggy and Leatherwood it meant that difference between want and even hunger. He led a gambler's life and abided by the gambler's creed. It was his belief that luck was a tangible element, impossible to analyze, impossible to define, but always a factor to deal with. Its coming and going could not be forecast. It was capricious, unpredictable, jealous. It was Vance's experience that when it smiled it must be appreciated, cajoled. A gambler who failed to recognize his good fortune and push the play usually found himself deserted by the fickle lady.

Lady Luck had not smiled on him lately. His stake, counting what Leatherwood had given him, was more than enough to pay the entry fee for the race the lean man had mentioned and leave enough, even if Rajah lost, to carry them along for a while. However, horses, even Rajah, were as unpredictable as Lady Luck and did not always run according to past performances.

Vance had bought the chestnut as a three-year-old for saddle use, along with its half-brother, which was a handsome, solid-hued chestnut that apparently had the makings of a racehorse. As it turned out, the blazeface Rajah proved to be exceptionally fast, and the half-brother finally won for himself the name of Rip Van Winkle because of his refusal to exert himself for any reason except to crowd his way into the feed trough.

Rajah had turned out to be their meal ticket at times when the cards ran the wrong way. In addition to being exceptionally fast over the short distances that were customary, the blazeface also had great endurance over a distance if allowed to set his own pace.

During the two years of ownership of the runner, Vance had learned the seamy side of racing. Doping, rough-riding, trickery of every kind were a part of the so-called sport of kings as it was practiced in the rough-and-ready contests at boom towns, mining camps and roundup wagons. Vance had learned to fight fire with fire. On several occasions the loafer, Rip Van Winkle, had been the torch.

Vance made his decision and walked to the poker table. He believed he had the two tinhorns measured, and felt they were no more anxious than himself to crowd the betting unless they felt they had top cards. He was sure he could handle Chick Nello. If he was reading Nello's actions correctly, the man was also playing with a limited bankroll, but trying to give the impression that he was in a position to push the play to the limit anytime he chose. Evidently, the Nello brothers had not prospered since the train robbery.

The house player was a different proposition. Even though he appeared to be handling the cards honestly during the short time Vance had been observing the game, he had all the means of crooked methods at his disposal if a big enough pot came along. Thus far the play had been small, cautious.

"Care if I sit in?" Vance asked as he reached the roped enclosure. A pot had just been raked in.

"Why not?" the house man said, indicating a vacant chair between the gray-haired man and one of the tinhorns. "I'm Barney. That's Mr. Burroughs to your left. An' Sid, Jimmy an' Bill."

"Howdy," Vance said. "I answer to the name of Vance. I'll buy fifty in chips as a starter."

The introduction had been acknowledged by nods and swift, cool, appraising stares from Burroughs and the tinhorns. The one Vance believed was Chick Nello, whose name had been given as Bill, merely grunted surlily.

Vance won the first pot. It only amounted to around ten dollars, for the house man was the lone player after the draw and did not challenge Vance's opening bet on a pair of queens. Vance dropped out early in the next three pots. The cards were running well for one of the tinhorns who answered to the name of Jimmy.

Vance filled three eights on the draw and won a pot in which Chick Nello stayed with two pairs.

"What did you say your name was?" Nello asked. He was edgy, his stack of chips low. Vance could see that the other players were wary of Nello. Two of the house troubleshooters were in the background. Apparently, Nello had a reputation as a troublemaker.

"Vance," Vance said.

Nello asked no more questions, but Vance knew he was being eyed speculatively at times. He wondered if Nello might have seen him somewhere in the past. More likely, Vance decided, Nello's brothers had passed along the word that the son of Jubal Barret had appeared in Gone Tomorrow, and Chick Nello was debating whether this might have any connection with his own reason for being here.

Vance lost two more pots, both of which he expected to win. He was debating whether to take his losses, which were still small, for he feared the cards were still running against him. Then he filled an inside straight and beat three jacks in Jimmy's hand. He won again, filling a diamond flush, this time against three aces and a straight. That fattened his stake.

He pushed the play. One of the tinhorns, Sid, finally shoved back his chair and cashed in the few chips he had left. The well-dressed Mr. Burroughs was growing flushed around the jowls. He probably could better afford to lose than any man at the table, but he was affable only in victory. Chick Nello's reactions were even more open to view. He was scowling and beginning to angrily slam down losing hands. He muttered profanity. He raised Vance three times, which was the limit, figuring he had a sure thing on a full house, but Vance had a higher hand of the same caliber with aces on top.

Nello almost exploded. The next pot was almost a repetition. When Vance met Nello's raise and boosted the ante, Nello almost rose from his chair. "You're four-flushin'!" he raged.

25

"It'll cost you another ten to find out," Vance said.

Nello furiously delved into a pocket, brought out a wrinkled bank note and tossed it into the pot. "I call you, fellow," he said, and spread his hand. He had a spade flush, jack high. Vance had a diamond flush, queen high, just enough to take the pot.

Vance, for a moment, believed Nello was going to go for his gun. The other three men at the table thought so also, for they skidded their chairs back in a panic, preparing to duck.

Vance also slid back his chair, so that his holster was clear, his gun in position to draw. But a hand closed on Chick Nello's arm. "Keep your hair on, mister," an authoritative voice spoke. "Don't start anything, or I'll finish it."

Once again it was the federal marshal, Ben Wheat, who had intervened.

"Keep your paws off me," Nello snarled, and jerked his arm out of Wheat's grasp.

"That's the thanks a man gets for maybe saving your life, my friend," Wheat said.

"My life?" Nello snapped scornfully. "You're being comical. I can take care of myself against the likes of a tinhorn like this one. Now, anytime. Day or night."

"So you think you're fast," Wheat said. "I tell you again that I just saved your bacon. It would have been self-defense on his part, for you were pushin' the play, asking for it. Now cash in your chips and walk out of here on your two legs, and be thankful. Don't start any more trouble in Gone Tomorrow, or I'll throw you into the stockade."

He added, "A tinhorn this one might be, my friend, but he's said to have already killed half a dozen fools like you. His name is Vance Barret. Maybe you've heard of him. And of old Jubal Barret."

Chick Nello did not answer. He cashed in what few chips were left in his cache and stalked out of the Buffalo Palace without giving Vance a second look. Vance also cashed in his chips. He was more than two hundred dollars ahead. He moved to the bar, tossed a dollar on the counter and said, "Beer. Make sure this time that it comes off the ice. In a bottle."

The barkeeper complied quickly. The beer, at least, was considerably colder than the previous purchase. Vance drank the beer, pushed past Ben Wheat, who lingered in the place, and walked out into the warm April sunlight. Chick Nello was not in sight.

Ben Wheat followed him and halted him outside the gambling house. "Keep clear of Bill Sands, Barret," he said. "I don't want any gun feuds in this town. Sands might hold a grudge against you and try to pay it off. Stay clear of him."

"Now, that's real considerate of you, Marshal, to be so concerned about my health," Vance said.

"I'm not concerned one little bit, one way or another, about your health," Wheat said. "But just take my advice and stay away from Bill Sands."

Two husky men had emerged from the nearby Buffalo Palace's swing doors, and had halted a distance away, one picking his teeth while he apparently listened to talk by the other. They wore hide boots, denims and cotton shirts, the typical garb of the boomers, but they did not exactly go with such costumes. They were studiously ignoring Vance and the marshal. Vance decided that they were Wells Fargo agents, and that they, along with Ben Wheat, had been in the gambling house to keep watch over Chick Nello.

"Who'd ever think that you'd act as guardian angel over Jubal Barret's tinhorn son," Vance said.

27

"I knowed your father," Ben Wheat said quietly. "He had me dead to rights once, after I'd hounded him a long ways. Could have killed me. He wasn't that kind. That's why I'm still alive. He was an outlaw, but he maybe had reason. The best you could ask for is to be half the man he was. Now move along. You're warned. Stay away from Bill Sands. Don't get mixed up in something you might regret the rest of your life."

Wheat walked away. The two husky men drifted off in another direction. Vance turned and found a girl standing in his path. Princess Delilah Fortune.

"Hello, there," she said. Her voice was sugary. Too sugary. She had just left the soothsayer's booth, for she still wore the spangled costume. She held a small parasol over her head, although the sun was mild.

"Howdy," Vance said very carefully.

"I was taken by the looks of that pretty blazeface gelding I saw you with a while ago," she said. "Do you happen to own the animal? Is he a runner?"

"I own him. I run him at times."

"They race here every afternoon, you know," she said. "They've cleared off a track out beyond the wagons. They run quarter, half mile. Sometimes longer. Do you aim to run him?"

"Maybe," Vance said.

"I bet he wins," she said. "I'd like to bet a whole dollar on him. What's his name?"

"Rajah," Vance said.

"He's got all the marks of a quick horse," she said.

Vance eyed her uneasily, sensing that she was not here merely to pose as a judge of horseflesh. "He's quick," he said.

"Are you going to ride him in the run for a claim?" she asked.

28

Vance grinned. "Hardly. I've got other aims."

"Would you sell that chestnut horse?"

Vance had not been prepared for this. He studied Princess Delilah more closely. He had taken it for granted that she was the usual type of medicine-show girl, hardened, cynical, knowing all the ropes, all the tricks, all the pitfalls. In addition, Leatherwood believed she was the sister of a man who had helped rob a train and commit murder. The paint on her cheeks, the rouge and powder on her lips, the blackened eyelashes and brows were the trademarks of women who followed a rough life. She bore these trademarks too brazenly, too falsely. On her, he sensed, they were a disguise rather than the stamp of a profession. Beneath the blackened brows were eyes of deep amber, very clear, very, very serious. Even desperate.

Disturbed, he was at loss for a reply for a space. "The horse is not for sale," he finally said.

"I'll give you five hundred dollars," she said. "Cash."

When she saw he was going to refuse, she said hastily, "Seven hundred. Seven hundred and fifty."

That was a fair price for a horse that raced for grubstakes in the back-country makeshift events.

"What would you use for money?" Vance asked.

She flushed beneath the paint and powder. "I'm—we're good for it," she said. "The saddlehorse we intended to use in the run went lame. As for the money, my father could buy and sell both you and your horse. You don't look like a millionaire to me. So it's a deal?"

"Of course it's not a deal," Vance said. "Don't try to stampede me. You're a long way from his price, even if I was of a mind to sell, which I'm not."

"A thousand dollars," she said, her voice shaking. "And I ought to have my head examined. But we do want to win a good claim."

"You realize, don't you, that your professor would have to sell a thousand bottles of that snake oil or whatever it is to make up for that price," Vance said.

"We'll do the worrying about selling the snake oil," she said. "You worry about seeing to it that you aren't trying to palm off a jughead on us."

"I'm growing a little befuddled," Vance said. "Wasn't it you who first came up with an offer to buy my horse?"

"We'll want to see your animal run before we put down any money, of course," she said. "My father won't take kindly to any sharper who tries to flimflam an inexperienced girl like me. I warn you that he's an expert at judging horses."

"And at judging flimflammers too, I take it, being in that business himself," Vance said.

"At least he knows how to deal with your kind," she said. "I haven't forgotten that the marshal warned you to get out of town. Are you going to enter that chestnut in a race this afternoon, so we can get a line on whether he's just a pretty shadow-jumper or can really run? It's got to be today if you expect to deal with us."

"Why the hurry? The run is days away."

"I want to have a chance to get used to the horse—also to see that he's rested and ready when the run starts."

"Do you mean to say you're going to make the run—saddleback?"

"Why not? My father is too heavy. And he's got rheumatiz. It won't be the first time I've been on a horse, I can assure you."

"Just for the sake of getting the record straight, I was really of a mind to put the chestnut in a race this afternoon if I could find a spot for him," Vance said. "But I'm not doing it to advertise him for sale. I tell you I have no mind for selling him."

30

"Every horse has its price," she said. "And every man."

"What sort of runners would Rajah be up against today?"

"Our harness stock could likely beat most of 'em. I hope your jughead has more getup in him. Likely, as I said, he's all looks and no bottom. A flashy quitter. On second thought, I doubt if he's worth much. Maybe not even a hundred dollars. I must have been crazy to have offered a thousand dollars without knowing what I was buying. I'm changing my offer. I'll say he's worth about one hundred. Maybe a hundred and fifty. We might not even want him at that price if he gets beat by those scrubs today."

"Well, well!" Vance exclaimed. "You learned your lesson well."

"What lesson?"

"How to be a horse trader."

"We'll discuss it after we see him race," she said.

She produced a small purse and extracted from it a silver dollar. "Put this on his nose if he runs," she said. "On a crowbait like that you ought to get good odds. He might even win if all the others bust their legs in gopher holes."

Then she was gone, hurrying back to the medicine-show platform. She looked back at him as she entered the fortunetelling booth. Vance held up the dollar and grinned. She smiled a little and vanished.

CHAPTER 3

Vance headed up the crooked street to find the pay corral Leatherwood had mentioned. His course carried him past the stockade where the sooners who

31

had been caught south of the deadline were held. There were forty or fifty men inside a barbed-wire enclosure patrolled by soldiers from an infantry company from Fort Reno who had been brought in to reinforce the cavalry. Some of the prisoners were playing cards, others merely sitting or lolling in the shade of the fly tents the Army had pitched to give them shelter. The majority likely would be released after the run had taken place. Others, more rebellious, like those in the Army wagons Vance had seen heading for Fort Smith, would be taken there for trial later.

With the deadline for the run approaching with each hour, Vance sensed the tension that was growing in this amazing ragtag stringtown. Some of the boomers had been here for weeks, as evidenced by the permanent appearance of some of the camps, but the majority were in little more than overnight bivouacs. The main river of incoming hopefuls was now at its peak. The prairie was alive with movement, and wagons could be seen stringing down from the north on the new trails. Gone Tomorrow's population was soaring by the hour, almost by the minute.

And so were prices. The pay corral proved to be a crooked circle of smooth wire stapled to branches of locust limbs that were set drunkenly in the earth. It was fitted with watering troughs, and stacks of hay were placed outside the fence, the feed being pitchforked over the wire onto the ground on which the stock foraged.

Leatherwood had kept both the runner and Pawnee clear of the cavorting and biting and kicking that was going on among some of the wilder stock in the enclosure by attaching grazing ropes to their halters and retaining control of them while he remained outside the wire. Seeing Vance approaching, he led his charges to

32

the gate, where the proprietor was backed up by an unkempt man who packed a brace of six-shooters and carried a shotgun under his arm.

"Thet'll be only ten dollars," said the proprietor, who was no model of cleanliness on his own part, and who was also heavily armed.

"You said it was only three dollars a hawss," Leatherwood complained.

"Thet was an hour or more ago," the man said. "Hay's gittin' more expensive every minute. Ten dollars, or I keep the hawsses 'til you pay up. An' I charge by the hour."

Vance paid. "Dog eat dog," he told Leatherwood. "Devil take the hindmost. Maybe we can catch him in a poker game later on and get it back. We're not aiming on being the hindmost. You had any grub lately?"

"Not lately. I cook my own. If I die o' gut-ache I want it to be of my own makin'. There're eatin' tents here and there along the line at three dollars a throw. Half-cooked beans and greasy razorback slabside. What do you reckon Iggy will have in the pot if I hold out 'til I find him? No more chili and beans, for Pete's sake."

"I wouldn't bet against it," Vance said. "Iggy thinks that he's a top hand when it comes to putting up a meal. I complained about his grub the other day, and he went off into the tules and sulked. I had to rustle up my own provender."

"Top hand? Why, he don't know how to cook nothin' but beans."

"At least it's free," Vance said.

"Free? For one thing, I'll have to listen to more of them stories about how he's such a stampede among the *señoritas* at whatever town he was last in. Then he'll try to thimblerig me into lettin' him deal a few hands o' monte at half a dollar a throw. If I ever find out how he switches the cards I'll skin him alive with a bullhide quirt."

"Your half dollars are safe today at least," Vance said. "There'll be no time for monte games. We've got other fish to catch. I wound up more than two hundred ahead in a small-limit game. I'd have done better if the marshal hadn't interfered."

"Interfered? Ben Wheat?"

"I almost tangled with the third Nello brother. Goes by the name of Bill Sands, as you said. He didn't take kindly to losing. He's all rawhide. Likes trouble. I thought I was going to have to draw on him. Wheat stopped it before it got too far. My hunch is that Wheat was in the Buffalo Palace to keep an eye on Chick Nello. He didn't want anything to happen to Nello, so he stepped in. I spotted a couple of other gentlemen hanging around who have the earmarks of Fargo agents."

"Sure," Leatherwood said. "It adds up. They trail the Nellos, the Nellos keep watch on the Judsons. It's like a dog chasin' its tail. Nobody has to draw you a map as to why they're all here, I reckon?"

And nobody had to draw Vance a map to tell him why the Judsons were so anxious to buy the blazeface runner. With eighty thousand dollars cached somewhere, a fast horse would be good insurance for reaching the hiding place ahead of the hordes of boomers who would roar across the deadline when the time came.

"Very interesting," Vance said. "But not for us. Now, how about these horse races? We could stand winning a little more money, and now we've got leeway to do some betting. Let the—"

"Eighty thousand dollars," Leatherwood said wistfully.

"Let the Nellos and the Judsons and the Fargoes work out their own problems," Vance snapped. "And Ben Wheat along with them."

"Eighty thou—"

"Keep your mind off things like that!" Vance said. "That money is prison bait, maybe gallows bait, and you know it."

"O' course, o' course."

"Don't be so damned butter-mouthed. You'll never quit listening for the owls to hoot, will you?"

"You're mighty pious for a feller what can second-card an' bottom-deal a poker deck, an' carries a ringer horse to gull the sharpers," Leatherwood said. "Since you're so danged pure o' heart, we could say thirteen thousand, instead o' eighty. Maybe you forget that there's ten percent to anybody what gits Wells Fargo its money back, an' the Santa Fe has offered a flat five thousand, dead or alive, for them that did the killin's."

"Do you, above all, really want any of that kind of money?"

Leatherwood's Adam's apple bobbed. He grimaced sheepishly.

"You called the turn. Your daddy must have rolled over in his grave at me bein' tempted by reward dinero. I just got to thinkin' how many Delmonico steaks I could buy with that kind of money at the Overland House in Kansas City. We might run a sandy now an' then on such people as are askin' for it, but there's a limit."

"Catch up your horse and ride out to find Iggy," Vance said. "Our luck is turning. I'll buy the Delmonicos in Kansas City, and it'll be in less than a

35

week if things go right. Send Iggy in with the wagon and Rip Van Winkle. Make sure Rip is dusted and mudded up to look disreputable."

"Whatever that word means," Leatherwood said. "Where will Iggy find you?"

Vance turned and peered toward the line of timber that marked the course of a creek a mile or so across the flats north of the deadline. The tilts of many covered wagons were visible among the brush, marking campsites of boomers. "See that wagon trail," he said, indicating a route that led to a ford in the stream. "Tell Iggy I'll hang up as close upstream from that ford as I can find room for the wagon. I'll take the chestnut down there and give him a rub. Now get moving."

Parting from Leatherwood, he mounted the roan and rode through camp, leading Rajah. He wanted to make sure the flashy blazeface was seen and talked about. Hundreds of boomers were camped here who soon would be depending on horseflesh to carry them to a desirable homestead ahead of others. A good horse might mean the difference between success or poverty in the years ahead. Not all would make the run saddleback. Many would cross the deadline in buggies or light wagons, depending only on single-harness animals. Others had heavy prairie wagons that would lurch along, drawn by teams. There were even ox wagons in the increasing assembly, their owners obviously depending on luck to win them a claim.

The race for the richest land would be among men in the saddle. Scores of horses were being exercised in the flats, their owners seeking to harden them for the test. Nearer at hand, horse-trading rings were busy, each attracting beehive interest. Horse lore was the topic of the day, the one subject of paramount interest.

The hour was noon, and the fragrance of meals being cooked arose from scores of wagonside fires. Vance was hungry, and was expecting to face a long afternoon before he would have a chance to eat again. There were eating tents along the way, but they were crowded, with long lines waiting outside. In addition, Leatherwood had warned of the quality of their offerings.

On an impulse, he turned back to the medicine show. The platform was empty, the curtain drawn over the entrance to the fortuneteller's booth. What listeners the professor had managed to attract had drifted away. The aroma of food being cooked drew Vance to the rear of the wagon. There a tent had been set up that served as a kitchen. Sidewalls extended out from the wagon, but the north face was open, looking out at the activity on the flats.

The Judson girl was busy over a wood range that had been set up, its stovepipe angling through a hole in the sidewall. She was stirring the contents of a Dutch oven in which was simmering what apparently was a stew. She had changed from the gilded costume into a cotton dress, and had a scarf tied around her dark-brown hair, and a gingham apron around her waist.

Her father was sitting listlessly on a camp stool. He had shed his frock coat and stovepipe hat, and slouched there, gazing unseeingly at his hands. In his attitude Vance believed there was something of the same desperation he had sensed in the girl when she had come to him to try to buy his running horse.

They turned swiftly, almost apprehensively, as he loomed up on the roan. "Howdy, Princess," he said, lifting his hat. "I caught a whiff of your cooking. They say a man is risking his life to eat at these beaneries where they charge plenty for serving up misery. I'd

37

much rather take a chance on what you've got in that pot, and I'll pay three dollars for it, and consider it a bargain."

He added, "If there's enough to spare, of course."

"Father, this is Mr. Barret, the man who owns the chestnut horse."

Henry Judson got to his feet. Instantly he was the big-framed, flamboyant, back-slapping medicine-show spieler once more. "My pleasure, sir," he said, coming to the stirrup to offer his hand. "Alight! Alight! Tether your animals to the wagon wheels and join us. There will be no charge. Honor us at the feast, humble as it is. I am Professor Schyler Fortune. This is my daughter, Delilah. And do not speak of paying. We—"

"The price will be two dollars," the girl said crisply. "In advance. I'm sure you can afford it. From talk I overheard, I understand you won money at poker in the Buffalo Palace this morning."

"News seems to get around in Gone Tomorrow," Vance said.

"I also understand you almost got into a gun fight there," she said. "What did you do—palm a pair of aces?"

"Worse than that," Vance said. "I was so lucky it got on one fellow's nerves, made him edgy."

He dismounted, tied up the horses. He produced two dollars, but she refused to accept the money. "Bet it on the chestnut along with the dollar I gave you if you can get the horse into a race," she said. "If you don't run him, you'll owe me three dollars. And I *will* want it back."

"I like to have everything spelled out in practical dollars and cents," Vance said. "Now that the financial arrangements are taken care of, I believe the coffee is

38

ready, if I'm any judge of aroma. I could use a cup to start with, Princess."

"My name," she said, "is Della Judson, not Delilah. My father's name is Henry Judson."

Vance was aware she was watching closely to see if the mention of their real names sparked a reaction in him. Evidently, she decided it had not, for she turned to rescue the coffeepot as it was about to boil over. She brought tin plates and cups, poured coffee and ladled food onto plates, placing the fare on a folding table.

"Sorry we did not bring along the china and silver," she said. "We didn't care to risk the royal plate in these parts. There are too many dubious persons around."

"I've always found it difficult to sleeve a silver platter," Vance said. "A fork or two now and then, perhaps, but they hardly pay. A platter is more awkward than palming a pair of aces."

Henry Judson chuckled. "Now that you two young people have crossed swords, let us be friends and eat in peace. I apologize for my daughter's attitude. She is very much set against gambling with cards. Perhaps with reason. Unfortunately, that pastime is one of my weaknesses, and not always with good results. That is why I sometimes turn to hitting the road with my medicine wagon. Now, what did you say was your name, my friend?"

His daughter answered, "This is Mr. Barret, Father. At least that's the name Marshal Wheat used in warning him not to make any trouble here in Gone Tomorrow."

"Barret it is," Vance said. "Vance Barret."

"Barret," Henry Judson repeated the name politely. Then it seemed to strike a nerve. "Barret!" he said again, and peered closer at Vance. He started to say more, but decided against it

39

His daughter was gazing questioningly at him. "Have you met Mr. Barret before?" she asked.

"No—no," her father said hastily. "It's just that I knew a man named Barret in the past. But there could be no connection."

"My father was Jubal Barret," Vance said. "I imagine that even if you never met him you have heard the name."

The girl turned, startled, staring at him. "Yes," Vance said. "The outlaw."

There was an awkward silence. Father and daughter traded glances. Then their manner changed, became more relaxed. "No matter, no matter," Henry Judson said briskly. "The sins of the father shall not be inherited by the son. Let us enjoy our repast together. I will now say grace."

It was Vance's turn to be surprised. Then he remembered that Leatherwood had said that Henry Judson had been a preacher in the past. He bowed his head, and was again surprised by the sincerity with which Judson pronounced the blessing.

They ate in silence for a time. The meal more than lived up to Vance's hopes. The main dish was flanked with home-baked bread, jam, pickles and dried apple pie.

"You ought to raise your sights," he told Della Judson. "This is a three-dollar meal. You'd make a good wife for some lucky man. He'd weigh three hundred pounds in no time."

"Is that intended as a compliment, or should I hit you over the head with a skillet?" she asked.

"My daughter tells me you don't plan to make the run, Mr. Barret," Henry Judson said.

"No. And you?"

Judson laughed wryly. "A medicine-show wagon is

hardly built for fast work, and we lost our saddlehorse some days ago. If we could induce you to sell that handsome chestnut gelding, it is possible we might be able to come up with a claim that would provide a home in the future for myself and my daughter."

"I don't plan on selling the chestnut," Vance said.

"Perhaps you might change your mind," Judson said.

In this busy camp many persons, both men and women, passed the tent. Vance watched two men saunter past, watched them glance into the open tent. They were the two brothers, Art and Lige. They moved on out of sight.

Vance studied the Judsons. They could hardly have escaped being noticed by the Judsons. He was right. Della Judson and her father traded glances, and Vance could see that the girl was especially disturbed, but attempting to conceal it. She began hurriedly preparing to wash the utensils.

Henry Judson offered a cigar, which Vance refused in favor of his own thin stogie. He watched Della Judson move about, doing the kitchen chores. She carried herself straight and firm. She had fire and mettle. She was shapely in the right places, rounded where it counted.

A drift of movement had set in past the wagons toward the flats. "They'll soon start racing," Della Judson said. "If you're going to enter your horse in one of the runs you ought to be getting down there, Mr. Barret."

"Vance is the name," Vance said. He shook hands with Henry Judson, thanking him for the hospitality. He offered a hand to the girl, but she pushed it aside.

"I might be forgetting myself and try to read your fortune," she said. "Fetch me back my three dollars—or the winnings."

"The chestnut can lose, you know," Vance said.

41

"There's no sure thing in racing—or in this life."

He mounted the roan and rode away, leading the blazeface runner. A distance out in the flats, a racecourse had been cleared of brush and high grass and leveled by fresno scrapers. Wagons and staked saddlehorses were clotted at one point, and more arrivals were adding to the gathering. A flatbed wagon, equipped with a sunshade, served as a stand for the placing judges at the finish wire. The last hundred yards of the stretch was roped off to keep spectators off the course.

Men were gathering around points where bets were being booked. In the background stood the tepees of Indian families. There were Osage, Pawnee, Cherokee and remnants of half a dozen other tribes around. They were seeing one of the last of their hunting grounds in the process of going into the hands of white men, but at this moment they were enjoying the spectacle, of which they were a colorful part, and were eager to enter their fast ponies against the mounts of the invaders. Inveterate gamblers, they were ready to back their entries with money, ponies, their personal possessions, and even their wives.

Riders and more wagons were arriving. Horses that were entered in the first race were being led up and down, some with blankets on their backs, others bearing only worn saddles.

A scurry of whooping cowboys rode past, yelling, fanning excited ponies with their hats. Set on hair triggers for fun, frolic or fight, they were from cattle outfits that had been ousted from the rich grazing of the promised land. They considered themselves suns and stars above the rank and file, whom they looked down upon as clods, sod-shakers and pig-sloppers. They had lived free, with no responsibilities, and could not visualize themselves grubbing out brush and bunch grass, or following a plowhorse to break sod.

They jeered at Vance as they rode past, classing him with the boomers. They were sure of themselves, for they had punched cattle in the virgin territory to the south of the deadline, knew the rich land of the creek bottoms, knew where wild turkey and deer were still as easy to take as quail and prairie hens.

They could not believe that these things were about to vanish, and that this land would soon be tamed. They were sure it would be the grangers who would disappear, and that they would again be able to ride free and long down there, drop their bedrolls wherever the notion took them, live off the land, sink their fishhooks in any stream and drag out delicious meals of perch or young catfish, or feast on venison or fowl. They brandished bottles. Their world was still young, and they could only look with scorn from their saddles at these hordes on foot who had come in, and were grinding the clean, rich grass of this land flat beneath their hideboot heels.

Vance returned the taunts and challenges with a grin and a wave of his hand. He could have told them that at the age of sixteen he had trailed north with a Texas herd as a button-boy wrangler with a remuda of rangy, wild cow ponies. He had seen swing riders brought in under blankets with Comanche arrows in their lungs, and he had jingled his spurs in the Long Branch Saloon in Dodge, where memories of Wyatt Earp and Bat Masterson were still vivid.

CHAPTER 4

REACHING THE SCENE OF ACTION, VANCE WAS directed to the promoter, Sam Dobbs by name, who had set up an office in a tent where the rules and regulations of the day's racing were posted. These were written in ink on pages that evidently had been torn from a ledger.

Vance studied the rules, which consisted mainly of warnings that no crooked work would be tolerated, and that once a horse was entered in any of the ten events on the afternoon's card, entry fees would not be refunded under any circumstances. Once a horse went to the post, it was officially in the race, even if it became incapable of running before the field was sent off. That meant that even if the animal dropped dead, his backers lost their bets, their entry fees.

The starter had the authority to recall the field and start the race over in case of unfair getaways. From past experience, Vance knew that this rule was a device by which an unwanted favorite could be worn out by repeated false starts in favor of some slower, less temperamental animal.

There seemed no limit to the number of horses that were allowed to enter each event. Already the first three races had more than a dozen entries scribbled on the lists, with notations that the fees had been paid. Prize money in these races was listed as twenty-five dollars to the winner, and five to the runner-up.

The conditions of the final and feature race of the day were listed in large black block letters. The prize would be one hundred dollars, winner take all.

Vance stood in line, back of boomers and two Osage Indians who were entering horses, and put down his entry fee. "Horse, Rajah II, chestnut with white blaze, white socks in front, Jockey, I. Espinosa," he intoned to Sam Dobbs, who was making a pretense of scribbling down the identifications.

Dobbs looked up. "Owner?" he asked.

"Vance Barret, Las Vegas, New Mexico," Vance said.

"You ever run your hawss here before, Barret?" Dobbs asked.

"No," Vance said. "I just got into Gone Tomorrow today."

"Ain't you the feller that near got into a gun ruckus in town a while ago?" Dobbs asked.

"It's my chestnut I'm entering in this race," Vance said. "Not me. I'm mighty slow over a quarter of a mile. And the chestnut won't be packing a gun. Fact is, he never packed one in his life."

Dobbs glared, then shrugged. "Your number will be seven, mister. That means you start in post seven. So far there's only seven horses entered in the feature race. We run our events on the level here. See to it that it stays that way."

"We see eye-to-eye on that, Dobbs," Vance said. "I don't take kindly to skullduggery. Fact is, I get mighty riled."

Betting was picking up. Ponies for the first race were being led down the course toward an overhead wire stretched between poles a quarter of a mile or so away, marking the starting line. There were about fifteen entries, and they were a colorful collection of Indian ponies with young Osages and Cherokees on pad saddles, and half a dozen cow ponies carrying young ranch hands. The field was rounded out by two ancient, sinewy animals with cagey, wizened riders aboard—typical followers of the uncertain matter of eking out a living in these sagebrush meets. Vance was sure these jockeys and their owners would be graduates in all the shady arts of foul, intimidation and doping. They lived in a world of wolf eat wolf.

The first race got off to a very ragged start, and was won by a young Osage on a wild, piebald pony. The victory aroused screeching jubilation among watching tribesmen and squaws. They carried the young rider off in triumph, then stampeded to collect the purse and cash in on bets. The profit from the wagering was far greater than the meager purse, but it was the purse the Indians were most proud of. Winning was the thing with them, particularly over the white man. Squaws were the most elated, their victorious screaming lasting long.

Vance left the racecourse, for it would be at least three hours before the feature event would go to the post, and led the chestnut runner across the flats to the quiet and coolness of the timber along the creek. The runner was excited, having heard the thud of hooves on the track and the cheering of the crowd. It sensed that it was going to race that day. The animal loved to race. Its eyes were beginning to hold the eagle glint of its thoroughbred strain. Vance rubbed it down with stream-soaked wads of grass, and it quieted.

He moved into the open at intervals to gaze around. Finally, he sighted a canvas-topped wagon of medium size approaching. It was drawn by a team of fine black Missouri mules. A horse slouched along back of it, tied to the tailgate. This animal was uncurried, dusty, with mud caked to its hock. Strap marks indicated it might have been used in harness or as a pack animal.

The driver of the wagon was Ignacio Guadalupe Espinosa. He sighted Vance's waving arms, stirred the mules into a trot, and tooled the wagon into the campsite

46

with a flourish. He alighted and swept off his steeple-crowned Spanish sombrero, which was adorned with silver bangles.

"So I am to guide the great chestnut *caballo* to victory on this day, *mi patrón,*" he said. "I trust you have been able to complete the arrangements. What will be my portion of the purse?"

"A kick in the britches if you lose," Vance said. "Ten percent when you win, and I'll credit it to all that *dinero* you've borrowed from me to blow in on the wenches."

"Was I the one who raised that gentleman to the limit in the *cantina* at Dodge City a few evenings ago with only two pairs against three tens, thereby depriving us of lodging beneath a roof for the night, and forcing us to camp like peons beneath a tree?" Iggy asked sorrowfully. "Was it—?"

"Never mind," Vance snapped. "I'll help you unhitch. You've done a good job on Rip, I admit. He never looked worse. And we've come to the right place. Everybody is out to make a dollar, fair means or foul. I've entered Rajah in the main race today. I put up twenty cartwheels to enter. First place pays one hundred. It's a skin game, of course. The promoter has a sure thing going for himself. But we stand to do all right too—if we win. Eighty dollars profit."

"And where did this twenty dollars come from, if I may be so impolite as to ask?" Iggy inquired. "You had ten dollars in your purse when you left Dodge City, of which two dollars and sixty cents belonged to me."

"Leatherwood's been playing pool and wedging into turkey shoots," Vance said. "I had a fair stake for sitting in a poker game. I got lucky. I'm going back to the track now to keep an eye on things. You hang out here until I come back for you. Keep Rajah's mind off racing. Get

47

your tack ready. If you ever rode to win, this is the time. Are you sober?"

"How could I be but sober with nothing in my pockets but memories?"

To make sure, Vance searched Iggy for possible hidden contraband. Iggy had an amazing genius for turning up, gay and singing, with feminine admirers clinging to his arms at inappropriate times.

Vance mounted the roan. "Don't go chasing after any of these sooner girls around here," he warned sternly as he rode away.

He rejoined the activity at the racecourse. The sixth run of the afternoon was under way. It proved to be a repetition of the earlier races, although the Indians were saddened when the judges gave a nose decision to a horse owned by a beefy man in a faded flowerbed vest and plaid coat. Vance was at the finish line and knew the decision was wrong. So did the Indians. They withdrew into a group, angry but helpless.

Vance was anxious to see what the opposition would be in the final race. The entry list carried the name of a mare named Lightning Flash, and its owners were listed as George and Henry Jones, the Nello brothers.

The ninth race was going to the post when he saw the brothers approaching. They were mounted, and leading a black mare which bore a light blanket. Riding double with one of the Nellos was a small, leathery man wearing a faded jockey blouse.

Vance judged that the mare was of Morgan stock. It had good, clean lines, with sturdy haunches and legs, and an intelligent head. It was evidently in good condition and rated respect on its looks.

Vance rode to the creek where Iggy lolled on his cot, plunking at a guitar. He had donned his boots and

48

breeches and a yellow blouse, on the back of which was sewn the eagle and serpent flag of Mexico, which had been the work of one of his feminine admirers.

"All right," Vance said. "Let's move in. I don't know much about the rest of the opposition, but there's a mare that might be hard to take into camp. She looks like she can run."

By the time they reached the track the odds for the feature race had been posted on a blackboard. Both the Nello mare and Rajah had been placed at even money. Sam Dobbs's oddsmakers were taking no chances on an unknown animal. When Vance tried to wager a hundred dollars on the chestnut to win, a hard-eyed man who was taking bets scowled. "Best I can do for you, mister," he said, "is one to two. That chestnut has got the earmarks of bein' able to cut the breeze. We don't like first-starters around here. We don't usually even take a bet on one 'til after it has run to show what it can do. I'm doin' you a favor, offerin' one to two."

Vance put his money back in his pocket. "I'd be loco to try to win fifty cents on the dollar on a gopherhole track like this, when I don't know what I'm running against," he said loudly. "Anything could happen on a layout like this—and likely will."

"Then stand aside and let men put down their money what ain't afeared of losin' it," the bookie said.

"My horse will beat these crowbait by ten lengths," Vance boasted. He walked angrily away, muttering, shouldering men aside. He was making himself known. He wanted it that way. He made a great show of giving Iggy the clenched fist sign and shouting, "Wire to wire, boy. Show 'em how a real horse can run."

Iggy followed instructions. He booted the blazeface into the lead in the first stride and opened up daylight

49

over the field before the dust of the start had swirled to its height. If any rough-riding had been in the minds of the other riders, they lacked opportunity. The black mare that had been entered by the Nellos managed to pull up within half a length of Rajah a hundred yards from the wire, but Iggy shook the whip in the eyes of the blazeface, and the horse responded, finishing a full length to the good. A third horse, a sinewy bay, was game, but no match for the mare or the chestnut

Iggy eased up his mount, which was still full of run, and headed back to the finish line. He removed his cap, waving it, and bowing to bystanders. He beamed on the flashy women who had come to the track in defiance of convention, for this was supposed to be a masculine world. He leaned from the saddle to pat the cheek of one of the most attractive. Rajah objected to such antics, pinwheeled, cathumped, and Iggy landed sprawling in the dust. He managed to cling to the reins, preventing a runaway until Vance arrived on the roan and calmed the horse.

"You clown!" Vance said. "I've never seen you look prettier than when you were flying through the air."

He led Rajah back to the finish line, with Iggy limping on foot in their wake. Men were clumped on the track, yelling, waving arms, and fists. The center of the group was Sam Dobbs and the two Nello brothers. Their rider had returned to the finish line, and had dismounted from the black mare. He bore his name in black letters on the back of his soiled blouse: RED BARNES.

Red Barnes sighted Vance and Iggy approaching, and came racing on foot to meet them. Iggy was his objective. "You crook!" Barnes snarled. "You penny ante thief! I'll teach you to steal a race from me."

He was upon Iggy like a tiger, swinging a fist. He had the advantage of weight over Ignacio Guadalupe Espinosa.

50

He also had the factor of surprise and momentum in his favor. His plan was to overwhelm Iggy and level him with a punch or two. His plan failed. Iggy had long since learned to defend himself. He sidestepped Barnes's rush, swung a left and right as his assailant went stumbling past. Both blows landed very solidly, the left to Barnes's jaw, sidewheeling him so that his solar plexus was an easy second target. Barnes kept plunging ahead and landed on the ground on his face, wheezing sickly. He lay still.

There was a moment of stunned silence. Then both of the Nello brothers burst into action. "You can't get away with this, fella!" the one with the flattened nose shouted. "Me an' my brother own Lightnin' Flash, an' we demand first money. Your leppie rider fouled our mare all the way from the start."

Vance dismounted. "In what way?"

"In what way? Everybody seen it. That cholo who rode your crowbait grabbed our boy's saddle blanket an' hung on at the start, throwin' our mare off stride. Then he quirted the mare across the face when she made a run at his horse."

Vance looked around. "Did anybody else see things like that?" he asked.

"I shore did," said a beefy, underslung man whose stomach supported a weighted gunbelt. "Your jock run as crooked a race as I ever laid eyes on."

"Did anybody else see this marvelous thing?" Vance repeated, looking around. "My horse came off the start a good length in the lead. Did anybody see my rider reach back eight feet and grab the mare's saddle blanket? Did anybody see him use a fifteen-foot bullwhip to hit the mare across the face when she was a length or more back?"

Guffaws arose. "Tell 'em, slim man!" a burly boomer yelled. "You won fair an' square. I had three dollars on your hawss, an' I aim to see that they pay up. Don't let

51

'em bully-rag you out'n your purse. We're on your side. There's been too much crooked work at this track already."

Scores of voices arose. "Pay up, Dobbs!" men shouted. "Pay up, or we'll wreck this here track and you too. The chestnut horse won clean an' honest."

The Nello brothers and Sam Dobbs and his gunmen were outnumbered. They mumbled protests, but didn't dare continue their claim. Dobbs sullenly counted out one hundred dollars from a wallet and handed the bills over to Vance. "Next time you run that horse, I'll see to it that you don't git away with anything, Barret," he said. "Us decent folk don't cotton to the likes of you an' that Mexicano you got ridin' for you. If we had any law around here he'd be put in jail for assault an' battery on that poor jockey, who might have a broken jaw."

"Let's hope it's not that trifling," Vance said, pocketing the money. "I expect to run the chestnut again—if the sign is right."

The day's races were over, and the spectators were scattering. Iggy mounted back of Vance on the roan, and they led the chestnut runner away at a walk to cool him.

Crossing their path on foot was a slim young person in jeans and denim jacket, with a felt hat pulled low. The face that looked up at Vance was not that of a boy but of a young woman—Della Judson She had not only defied convention by attending the races, but had added to the impropriety by disguising herself in masculine attire. Vance gave her a scowl that told her what he thought of such boldness.

He failed to chasten her. She gave him an impish wink and a toss of her head that told him where he and his scowls could go for all she cared.

"Was that not the *señorita* who was so impudent as to wink at you?" Iggy breathed as they rode on.

"You didn't see anything," Vance growled.

"And wearing pantaloons like a boy?"

"You *were* seeing things."

"I could not be mistaken, *señor.* I am an expert in such matters. She was very attractive, even though she was dressed to conceal that fact. What a waste! I am of a mind to follow her, and—"

"You're of a mind to see to it that Rajah is rubbed down, watered, fed and watched every minute. Those two warthogs who call themselves the Jones brothers—which isn't their real name—aren't exactly the usual run of gypsy horse owners. That's only a cover for something else. They have a natural talent for trying to pick up a few dollars here and there by any means that comes to mind— as they just demonstrated."

"You are trying to tell me something, *señor.*"

"I'm trying to tell you to keep your eyes open. They're the kind who'll try to see to it that Rajah can't run a lick the next time we start him against their mare."

Iggy uttered a cackle of mirth. "Oh, ho, ho! I see. Oh, *amigo,* but you are the sly one. You have set them up for the kill, like the ducks on the pond. Should we make the switch at once—tonight?"

"Of course not. We've got to play this cozy. They might not fall for it. Particularly so, if we seem too anxious."

They cooked and ate a supper, with venison that Iggy had bagged en route to Gone Tomorrow as the main fare, along with biscuits from the Dutch oven and tinned tomatoes.

"Do you have to put hot peppers even in tomatoes?" Vance complained, hurrying to the creek to cool his burning throat.

"They are very good for the health," Iggy said. "They keep away all types of sickness."

"There are easier ways to die," Vance said.

"There are some who think I am a very good *cocinero*," Iggy said, aggrieved.

Vance thought of the meal Della Judson had prepared. "You have a few things to learn," he said. "And it wouldn't do any harm if you took a bath now and then."

"But, *señor*, I do," Iggy moaned. "You have always insisted on it."

"You smell like a horse—or a mule."

"That is not confined to myself," Iggy pointed out. "We cannot live with horses and mules and smell like violets."

Vance glared fiercely at him. "Are you trying to say that I smell like a horse?"

"If I answered that truthfully we might come to blows," Iggy said.

After the meal was finished, Vance opened the pack in which he carried his belongings, got out his shaving kit and clean garments. He heated water, then, using their small mirror, shaved by the uncertain light of their oil lantern and the flickering campfire. He went to the creek, stripped and lathered himself, then plunged into the stream. He uttered moans of agony, for the water was icy cold at this early season. He emerged, toweled himself, dressed, and was very careful with the necktie he donned as he stared into the mirror.

Iggy watched all this with growing suspicion. "Cleanliness is next to godliness, so it is said," he finally observed. "You are surely bound for heaven, *mi patrón,* after this night's effort. If I am not mistaken, you shaved and bathed only this very morning before setting out to ride to this place when we were camped on this same stream north of here."

"So what?" Vance growled.

54

"And now you have gone through the torture once more. Surely it was not my innocent remark about smelling like a horse that induced you take such measures. You are not in the habit of heeding the wisdom I offer you."

"If I listened to all the hokum you put out; I'd be in the boobyhouse," Vance said, scowling at the necktie, and reknotting it in an attempt at a new and more dashing effect.

"Would I be considered rude if I inquired the name of the *señorita* who has aroused your interest?"

"Shut up."

"Would this person happen to be the *bonita muchaha* wearing pantaloons, who made the rogue's eye at you so recently?"

Vance laughed down such a thought with scorn. "Now that you mention it, it happens that I've got to look up the young lady and give her back three dollars that she asked me to bet on Rajah this afternoon."

"Three dollars? I see. Or perhaps I do not see. Am I to understand that this person came up to you and gave you this money to make the wager?"

"Not exactly. It's Rajah, not me, that she's after. She and her father want to buy him to ride him in the run. She offered a thousand dollars for him."

Iggy's eyebrows became pointed arches. "And you refused?"

"Of course."

"But *señor*, in view of our reduced circumstances, that would be a very nice stake. The future of a racehorse is very uncertain, as you know. Sound today, and lame tomorrow."

"Don't try to hurrah me. You'd never forgive me if I sold that horse. You treat him as though he was your

55

brother. In addition to that, where would we find another horse to match up with Rip Van Winkle? All the fun would go."

"You are right, of course," Iggy said. "I regret that I permitted greed for money to cause me to forget other things for the moment. But it was a good price. This *señorita* must desire our *caballo* very much. She may offer other inducements. Be wary, *amigo,* or both of us may be afoot, and this *muchacha* will no longer need to use the rogue's eye for you, for she will have what she wants."

"I wasn't born yesterday," Vance snapped. "No woman can twist me around her finger. I might play a little poker tonight if I can find the right game again. I've got a stake big enough now to tackle the tough ones. I felt my luck come in today. Maybe a thousand dollars will look like mice bait to us before long."

"See to it that you only play poker," Iggy said. "And not with fire."

CHAPTER 5

VANCE SADDLED THE ROAN AND RODE INTO THE HEART of Gone Tomorrow, where torchlight flared along the gambling line. Henry Judson was booming out his spiel from the platform of the medicine show. His leather-lunged sales talk rolled along mechanically, but he watched Vance ride up, and gestured toward the kitchen at the rear.

There, Vance found Della Judson completing the kitchen chores after the evening meal, wearing the gingham apron over her spangled skirt, in readiness for resuming her role as Princess Delilah. Moths battered at the globe of the lantern overhead, small crimson shafts of firelight darted from around the stove lids on the coal range where the evening cookfire was dying. The tent was sweetly pungent with the odor of yeast in a crock, and of bread freshly baked.

She motioned him to dismount, and poured coffee into a tin cup. When he extended three silver dollars she would only accept one. "I only had the courage to risk a dollar," she said. "And I don't charge for feeding wandering persons who drift by in need of help."

Vance tested the coffee and set it aside to cool. "You shouldn't have gone down there this afternoon, you know," he said. "You were lucky you got away with it. There are rough characters around racetracks."

"I just love to watch horse races," she said. "Why is it that men are supposed to have all the fun?"

"I spotted you for a girl. So did Iggy, my jockey. There might have been others."

"But nothing happened," she said.

A man walked by the open end of the tent, dimly reached by the lamplight. He proceeded on into the darkness, apparently with no more that a casual glance in their direction. He was one of the Nello brothers, Lige.

"Like that one," Vance said.

"Why do you say that?" she asked.

"Have you seen him before?"

A small pucker appeared between her eyebrows. "I saw him at the races today. Wasn't he one of those who accused your rider of fouling the black mare?"

"Is that the only time you recall seeing him—or his brother? They go by the name of Jones."

He was trying to determine whether or not the Judsons were aware of the identity of the Nellos.

"Would you like a touch of canned milk in the coffee?" she asked abruptly. "That'll help cool it so it won't blister your tongue."

"I will, thanks," Vance said. He studied her from under his hat brim as she cooled the coffee and stirred it. It was obvious that she had decided to change the subject. Henry Judson's voice was booming from the platform. Vance listened critically. He was thinking that, like the girl in her spangles and painted lips and beaded eyelashes, Judson was overdoing his role. The two Judsons were tense and overacting. The activity of the camp ebbed and crested around them. Someone was driving tent stakes nearby. At a neighboring wagon, men were in a half-angry dispute over a missing tool. Banjos and guitars tinkled here and there in the early darkness. A man with a Deep South accent sang a spiritual in a strong bass voice. From the gambling line came the droning medley of barkers' voices, of men in their cups at the bars, of laughter, of conviviality. Wagons creaked by. Galloping horses' hooves clattered as riders passed down the way.

Vance watched Della Judson hang the dishpan on a pole. She removed the apron and the scarf she had wrapped around her hair. She was preparing to return to her role as Princess Delilah, the palm reader.

He debated whether to tell her that he knew about her brother and about the Nellos. More to the point, he wanted to warn her about the Wells Fargo agents and Ben Wheat. There was such a thing as being an accessory to a crime—particularly where murder was involved.

More passersby drifted by, some near at hand, others at a distance, barely touched by the lantern light. Vance took note of one, a husky man garbed as a boomer. He was one of the pair he had tabbed as Wells Fargo agents.

"What are you thinking about?" Della Judson asked.

"Should I be thinking about anything in particular?" Vance inquired.

"I'm hoping you are considering our offer."

"Offer?"

"To buy your runner. That was the main reason I went to the track this afternoon. To see if your blazeface could run and seemed sound. You said you didn't intend to run for land. We are very anxious to win a good claim. With a horse like that we'd have a good chance."

"I'm afraid the answer is still no," Vance said.

He saw hope die in her, saw the desperation return. Dreariness came to him. How could money mean so much to this girl? Tainted money at that.

"There must be other horses that can be bought," he said. "Have you tried?"

"Yes," she said tiredly. "But you ought to see the kind that are offered for sale. Broken-down animals that would likely play out in the first half mile. Any really good horse is worth the price of a claim at this moment. We can't take a chance on—"

She broke off as though realizing she had ventured onto dangerous ground. What she had almost said, Vance reflected grimly, was that it wasn't a matter of merely winning a farm, as far as she and her father were concerned.

"We'll give you two thousand dollars for the chestnut horse," she burst out abruptly. Before Vance could answer, she said, "Twenty-five hundred dollars."

She stood taut and pallid, awaiting his answer. She was expecting surprise in him, even suspicion, and questions that she did not intend to answer.

Vance did not ask those questions. He already knew the answers. He placed the empty coffee tin on the table, and said, "Good night."

She caught his arm as he turned to leave. "Please!" she breathed. "What is the price?"

"Don't you understand?" he said. "I'm doing you the biggest favor possible in this world. I'm saving you from yourself. Saving your life."

He left the tent, mounted and rode aimlessly through the swirl of the camp. Twisted shadows danced against the banners of the dancehalls, against the sides of wagons, against the faces of men as the torches blazed and flickered in the night wind.

More boomers were still pouring in, blundering through the darkness beyond the wagons in search of grass for stock and room to pitch camp for the night. The dancehalls and gambling traps were in noisy operation.

Vance was taking a new and long look at the one person he knew best, and still did not know. Himself. He had been entertaining a professional, sophisticated scorn for these newcomers who intended to root themselves into the soil and flourish there like trees, like the corn and wheat they would sow. They'd grub out a living day by day, month by month, year by year. They'd battle nature, blizzard and whirlwind, grasshopper and drought. They'd grow old and gnarled along with the trees in the orchards they'd plant. Some would grow ripe and rich, like the wheat that would spring up from their fields. They'd marry and live out full lives here, and die, with their children inheriting the earth they had tamed, with their widows wearing black silk and left to mourn them.

And who would mourn Vance Barret? And where would his grave be when his time came? He tried to

60

drive such vaporings out of his mind, tried to reassure himself of his superiority over these people and their prospects of such a drab and placid existence.

His was a different world. His world was one of the nimble finger and fast dollar. His law was the law of the pack. There were no mourners for those who fell. Ben Wheat was one of his world, hard, unyielding, packing guns that could and had killed. And Iggy, the swaggering jockey, whose cherished ambition had been to be a toreador in the great ring at Mexico City, but who was, instead, a drifting gypsy who followed the cowtown rodeos and racetracks to pick up a few dollars by fair means or by trickery. And there was Jim Leatherwood, whose heart and interest was still with the men of the owlhoot trail.

These were Vance's people, the inhabitants of his world with its frame of frayed tinsel. Even the Nellos were part of it. They were outlaws, as had been Vance's father and brothers. But there the similarity ended. The Nellos were also murderers. That crime had never been part of Jubal Barret's wildness.

Della Judson had appeared on the platform of the medicine show and was banging a tambourine. Her presence was attracting a drift of onlookers, ostensibly to listen to her father's spiel, in reality to gaze at her. Anger suddenly seethed in Vance. Why did she cheapen herself that way, displaying herself before the eyes of these men?

He knew the answer. Money. Stolen money. A lot of it. The medicine show was only a cover for the real purpose the Judsons had in being in Gone Tomorrow.

He swung around and entered the Buffalo Palace. The high-play table was in operation, but its six chairs were taken. He could see that the stakes were steep. He suddenly had no wish for stiff play at this time, and moved toward a stud table where only four players sat, and where the game appeared leisurely.

None of the Nellos was in the place. He was intercepted by one of the hard-eyed gunmen who acted as troubleshooters and bouncers for Johnny Briscoe. "No trouble tonight, fella, if you set in on a game," the man warned him. "I was here this mornin' when you almost got into a gunfight."

"If a gunfight comes," Vance said affably, "I'll let you do all the shooting. Except at my back. Now stand out of my way."

The man appraised him, then moved aside. He was experienced at picking out the tough ones from the run of the trade. "One warnin' is all we give, you know," he said. "I ain't alone. There are two or three more like me what work for Johnny, in case I need help. Be peaceful."

"I never started a ruckus in my life," Vance said. "I only end them."

He moved on and inquired if he might sit in at the stud game. The players had seen the byplay with the troubleshooter, and eyed him dubiously. They finally nodded reluctantly.

It was a careful game for a time. Finally, Vance's opponents relaxed. Although Vance won his share of pots, they began to realize it was only a friendly game to pass time. None relished losing, but it was a contest of cards and skill, with no house player involved, and the stakes modest.

After about an hour, Vance saw Jim Leatherwood enter the gambling house. Leatherwood strolled to the bar. He gave no sign that he was aware of Vance's presence, but lingered there, a foot on the brass rail, sipping beer. Presently, he began tossing dice with another patron, with the price of the beer as the stake.

Vance looked at his watch. He was less than twenty dollars ahead of the game. "I'm going to cash in my chips," he said. "I'm bushed, and I'm heading for the blankets. I'll likely be around tomorrow night if you gentlemen want to try to get your money back. I warn you I'm in a lucky streak. But if you really want to win a little spare cash, take all bets on my horse Rajah if he starts in a sprint again. He's in top shape."

"You aimin' on racin' him ag'in?" one of the men asked.

"If I can find a spot for him," Vance said. "All he needs is a day's rest. Well, good night, gentlemen."

He left the Buffalo Palace and strolled toward the hitchrack alongside the building where he had tied up his horse. Johnny Briscoe hired armed guards to watch over the mounts of his guests to see that they were not stolen, and Vance tossed a half dollar to the man who patrolled the area where he had left the roan.

Leatherwood came from the gambling house and joined him in the darkness.

"All set?" Vance murmured.

"Yeah," Leatherwood answered. "When should I start my pitch?"

"As soon as you figure it's the time," Vance said. "Work on the Nellos. They're ripe for it. It's always the smart ones that fall the hardest for a skin game. They're not only crooked themselves, but they're hard losers. And they're in cahoots with the leppies that operate that racetrack."

"They sure are," Leatherwood said. "That beer-belly with the black mustache what calls himself Sam Dobbs rode the long trail with the Nellos a time or two. He likely still does when he ain't runnin' crooked races in the sagebrush."

"That further eases my conscience," Vance said.

"What conscience is that?" Leatherwood asked.

"You have a sharp tongue, tall man. Sharks are for the catching. They always swallow the bait, hook and sinker."

They parted. Vance again was about to mount when another man walked out of the darkness and said? "One minute, Mr. Barret."

The arrival was Henry Judson. He evidently had hurriedly left the platform, for he was wearing his frock coat and rusty stovepipe hat.

"I want to renew our offer to buy your racehorse," Judson said.

"I've tried to make it clear that the horse is not for sale," Vance said.

"Just what is your price?" Judson asked.

It was on the tip of Vance's tongue to put the amount at eighty thousand dollars, just to see Judson's reaction. But he refrained. "It's no use," he said. "You're wasting your time. You should try somewhere else, Mr. Judson."

"Three thousand dollars," Judson said hoarsely.

"Are you serious?" Vance demanded.

"Very serious," Judson rasped. "Very!"

"For that kind of money you could have your pick of any horse along the deadline."

"I haven't time to try," Judson said. "Your horse is the one we want. We've seen it run, know it is a sound horse."

"I'm sorry. Can't you understand—"

"Four thousand dollars!" Judson said.

"You mean you'd actually pay money like that for the runner? It must be a mighty nice piece of land you've got your mind set on."

"It is."

"You have that much money on you?"

Henry Judson hesitated. "I can get it," he said. In him was again the desperation Vance had seen at times in both father and daughter.

"You mean you haven't got it—the cash?"

"You will be paid," Judson said earnestly. "I'll pledge my life on that."

"Four thousand dollars is quite a wad to raise in a hurry," Vance said. "Just where would you get it?"

Judson started to speak, then held it back. Vance believed he had been on the verge of making a revelation, but had decided against it. "I can get it," Judson finally said. "You will have to take my word of honor on that."

Vance was silent Judson said bitterly, "I'm aware that the word of honor of a medicine-show faker can hardly be regarded as reliable security. But, it's the best I can offer—and it is an honest offer, believe it or not."

"Do you know something," Vance said. "I believe you. I believe you'd get me the money somehow. But I can't take it."

"What? Good God, man! Why not? Do I have to get down on my knees to you? Just what do you want of me?"

"Take your daughter out of this—"

Knifing through the throb of activity around them came the wild, terrified scream of a girl. It came again.

Vance was in the saddle and spurring the roan away before Henry Judson could move. That scream had come from the direction of the medicine show.

Men were racing in the same direction, but Vance outdistanced them. He hit the ground in a running dismount at the opening into the kitchen tent. Della stood in the kitchen. The lantern wick had been turned low to conserve kerosene while she was on the platform. In its dim light her face was ghastly white beneath the paint and powder. Her hair had been torn loose. A sleeve of the spangled dress was ripped to the shoulder, revealing a bruise on her upper arm.

"What happened?" Vance asked.

"It—it was a man," she chattered. "He was in the wagon, searching for—for money, I suppose. I had been out front telling fortunes, and came into the wagon and surprised him. I tried to stop him, but he was too strong, too rough. He ran away into the darkness."

Her father arrived, along with a swarm of curious boomers. "Did you know the man?" Vance asked. "Could you identify him?"

"All I know was that he had on a bandana mask, and his hat was pulled low. It was too dark to see anything clearly in the wagon."

One of the boomers spoke. "There was more'n one of 'em. I saw two fellers runnin' away after you hollered, ma'am. One of 'em cut past my wagon, but I didn't git much of a look at him in the dark. I heard somebody runnin' off in the opposite direction."

"I saw only one," Della Judson said.

Her father mounted the steps into the wagon. Vance, standing at the steps, peered into the wagon. In the faint light he could see that Henry Judson was kneeling beside a sizable leather trunk. This stood beside a cot which was curtained off from what evidently was his daughter's sleeping quarters.

Clothing was scattered on the floor in disorder. Henry Judson seemed searching for something deep in the trunk. Suddenly he seemed to relax, for he straightened, and Vance heard him utter a sigh of vast satisfaction and pocket something he had found.

He looked around, discovering that Vance had been watching. "They—they got nothing of consequence," he said. "Della must have interrupted them—him—in time."

Judson descended from the wagon. "Just a sneak thief," he told the bystanders. "He got nothing, as far as I can see. Thanks, folks, for hurrying to help my daughter. I doubt if we'll be troubled again. The Princess Delilah has a scream that carries for a considerable distance. No man would want to turn that loose twice, I imagine."

The arrivals laughed, and began to drift back to their wagons. Petty stealing was commonplace in Gone Tomorrow. Each night there had been shootings and stories about robberies. A few had been exiled from camp on threat of having necks stretched if they returned. There was talk of organizing vigilantes to deal with the rough element.

Vance lingered. "Want me to hang around?" he asked. "I could fetch my bedroll and do my snoring here."

"No, no!" Henry Judson exclaimed. "That won't be necessary. Our visitor won't be back. It amounted to nothing."

"Then I'll say good night," Vance said.

He moved to where the roan stood, reins trailing. Judson came hurrying to overtake him. "About your horse . . . ," the man began.

"I'm going to run him again in a race, if possible," Vance said. "He might go lame, break down. Horses do that, as you well know."

"Then you *are* considering selling him to us?"

"Do I understand that your daughter intends to make the run if you can find a horse for her?"

Judson shrugged. "She's younger, much lighter."

"From the looks of the mob that's gathering, it's going to be quite a scramble. It won't be a place for a woman. She might be killed."

"You're right," Judson said. "I'll make the ride myself. Does that influence you to accept my offer?"

"I'm not sure," Vance said. "But I can't say why I'm caring a hoot whether either of you live or die."

He left Judson standing there astonished, mounted and rode away. He sat wearily in the saddle, letting the horse pick its way across the flats, avoiding hummocks of brush and other pitfalls. He was seeing again Henry Judson's frantic search in the leather trunk, and the man's obvious intense relief when he found that what he had been seeking was still in place.

Obviously, the intruders had not been mere sneak thieves. They were the Nello brothers, and what they had been seeking was in the trunk. But they had not found it. It could not have been money or valuables they were after. What they had been hunting must have been some clue to the location of the missing train-robbery money. The only logical conclusion was that the Judsons were in possession of a map, and the Nellos knew of its existence.

CHAPTER 6

IGGY WAS SITTING BY THE CAMPFIRE, PLAYING solitaire with a thumbed deck of cards, when Vance reached their wagon. He finished the game while Vance took care of the roan, then swept up the cards. "The luck?" he asked cautiously. "It did not stay with you, after all? You lost the *dinero* once more?"

Vance loosened his tie and shirt in preparation for turning in. "What was that, Iggy? Oh, the game. What makes you think I lost?"

"Ah, so you did not lose. You won? How much?"

"Only about twenty dollars. I only sat in a small game for an hour or so. I was waiting for Jim to show up."

"Then it is that the bath in the cold water and the dressing up was wasted," Iggy said. "That is why you wear the frown, and why your mind is so far away."

"What are you talking about?"

"The object of your affections did not respond, I take it. Do not be downhearted. There are many, many other *señoritas* in this world, *amigo.*"

"You do run off at the mouth, don't you?" Vance snarled. "If there's anything that gravels me, it's a smart-tongued know-it-all who doesn't know anything."

He walked out of the wagon circle to where their stock was picketed. The two mules stood hipshot and dozing. Rajah moved nervously, its white stockings and forehead blaze catching the glint of the firelight. It bore a blanket on which its name was done in gold threadwork—another gift from one of Iggy's feminine conquests. Rajah's companion was the dusty, uncurried animal that had come into camp on a hackamore rope at the tailgate of the wagon, Rip Van Winkle.

He returned to the fire and continued preparations for turning in. He looked up at the sky.

"It will be all right to sleep in the open tonight," Iggy said. "There will be no rain. I, however, will sleep in the wagon. It is warmer. But you have the more fat, and . . ."

"Fat?"

"Only by comparison," Iggy said hastily. "You will not let me eat all the food I prefer. Always it is my weight that you talk about. I cannot have this, or cannot

69

have that. The tamales, the frijoles, the tortillas. In Dodge there was a fine Mexican family whose daughter cooked the most delectable—"

"You can fatten yourself up next winter. Right now I don't want Rajah to carry a load of frijoles and tortillas whenever you get aboard."

"I will continue to starve," Iggy sighed. "I trust that will make you happy. And I trust it will not be for long."

"The day after tomorrow, I hope," Vance said. "That will be about our last chance before the land rush. Are you stocked up on whitewash and brown coloring? Did you let anyone in Dodge know what it was for?"

"Not even the prairie dogs," Iggy said. "Then I may look forward to indulging in a few drinks tomorrow evening."

"No. You'll only pretend to be drunk, you hear me. I don't want Rajah carrying a hangover either."

"Just one little drink, *por favor, señor. My* throat, it needs it. It is very dry. And, as you know, I am a very, very poor actor. How can I make them believe I am drunk if I am not drunk?"

"You've had enough experience to know all the ropes," Vance said. "If our luck holds tomorrow night, I might be able to run our stake up to five or six hundred. Maybe more. A lot more."

"A lot more? What is it you are trying to tell me, *mi patrón?* I would say that there is not much more money than that in this whole place."

"I'm wondering what people like you and Leatherwood and me would do if eighty thousand dollars fell into our laps?"

Iggy halted, a boot half off, and stared. He realized that Vance was serious. "*¡Hola! ¡Madre Dios*! Then I could get very drunk indeed. But I do not follow you. Is it a bank that we are going to rob?"

70

"Forget it, Iggy," Vance said. "I was talking through my hat. Forget it."

He refused to talk any more, regretting that he had spoken. He lay for a long time before falling asleep. A fierce anger burned in him. An anger against Della Judson. He kept twisting and turning. He kept seeing a horrible vision of her in a prison uniform, her hair growing gray, her features coarsening with the years. He found his fists tight-gripped, palms sweating.

"The little fool!" he burst out in agony.

In the wagon Iggy sat up, voicing alarmed questions.

"Go to sleep," Vance snarled. "You're dreaming."

Playing poker the next night in the Buffalo Palace at the same low-limit table, Vance saw Jim Leatherwood, apparently gay and flushed with drink, come swaggering into the place, accompanied by, of all persons, Art and Lige Nello. Chick Nello was also in the gambling house, playing at a stud table, but, as before, staying apart from his brothers.

And, true to Vance's expectation, two of the men he believed were Wells Fargo agents soon wandered in. They studiously avoided giving any indication they were in the least interested in the Nellos.

Leatherwood and the Nellos spent some time at the bar, drinking and rolling dice. The Nellos spotted Vance. Lige came barging to the table. Leatherwood and Art followed, leering drunkenly.

"You're the fella what owns that chestnut runner what went up ag'in our mare the other day, ain't you?" Lige Nello said.

"That's right," Vance replied.

"Wal, we ain't a danged bit happy about the way that race was run, an' we figger you owe us another chance

71

to show that our Lightnin' Flash mare kin beat that crossbred horse of yours, goin' away. Ain't I right, boys?"

His brother and Leatherwood loudly attested that he was correct and that he was entitled to a rematch.

"Anytime," Vance said. "Name the day."

Lige grinned and looked slyly at his companions. "How about tomorrow afternoon?" he asked.

"I'm agreeable," Vance said. "For what purse?"

"Purse? To hell with a purse. We'll make this a match race. Maybe Sam Dobbs will put up fifty dollars or so to the winner, just because he's got sportin' blood in him. But this'll be between you an' us Jones brothers. I got a hundred dollars what says our mare kin kick dust in the face of your jughead."

"A hundred dollars?" Vance laughed tolerantly. "You haven't really got much faith in your mare, have you? How about five hundred?"

He was bluffing. Every cent he and Leatherwood and Iggy possessed came to a little more than three hundred dollars. But he believed the Nellos were none too affluent either. He had judged correctly Lige Nello's bet had been raised, and he found it beyond his means to call. His scarred face reddened with anger, but he had to hedge.

"How about two hundred?" he said weakly.

Vance turned back to the poker game. "I'll enter my horse in the feature race and bet on him," he said. "I can make more money that way."

"Three hundred!" Nello squeaked.

"All right," Vance said. "Three hundred it is." He drew out his wallet and casually began counting out the money, making sure that the onlookers did not see that this just about cleaned him out. "Let Johnny Briscoe hold stakes. Is that satisfactory to you, Mr. Jones?"

Lige wanted to refuse, but could not think of reasonable grounds on the spur of the moment. "It's all right with me," he said lamely. "I don't carry that much money on me in a place like this, but I'll get it within an hour or so."

A person who appeared very intoxicated came staggering into the Buffalo Palace, singing a romantic Spanish song in a loud voice. He paused, swept off his huge sombrero and bowed low. This sent him staggering headlong into a bystander, who seized him, straightened him and steadied him on his feet.

"*Muchas gracias, amigo,*" the arrival said, beaming. He was Ignacio Guadalupe Espinosa, and it seemed that he was very much in his cups, in spite of Vance's warning.

He glared owlishly around, then advanced to the bar. "Tequila!" he shouted grandly. "For everyone."

The barkeeper scowled. "We don't handle none of them foreign boozes," he said. "Furthermore, you likely couldn't pay for it even if we had it."

Iggy drew himself up proudly. "You insult the son of a grandee of old Mexico," he stated. "I will remember this."

He turned and started to stalk out of the place with great dignity. He did not make it to the door. His knees suddenly caved in, and he collapsed into the sawdust, beginning to snore lustily.

Vance arose and said to the other players, "I'll have to cash in. That's my jockey. But it looks like I'll have to get another rider tomorrow."

He walked to the supine Iggy and tried to shake him into wakefulness. "*Estúpido!*" he growled. "I told you to stay in camp tonight."

He slung Iggy over his shoulder and walked out of

73

the Palace. Henry Judson was making his spiel on the platform of the medicine wagon down the way, and his daughter stood at the door of the fortuneteller's cubby. Vance carried Iggy, who was babbling his romantic song, down the street to the medicine show and around to the kitchen. Della Judson left the platform and came through the wagon to join them.

"Sorry to inflict this on you," Vance said.

"He's drunk," she pronounced.

Vance sat Iggy on his feet. Iggy had managed to keep his sombrero on his head. He once more removed it and bowed low to Della. "Ah, the beautiful *señorita*," he gushed. "I am charmed."

"Would you mind letting him sleep it off here?" Vance asked.

"Why here?"

"It's a little far back to camp," Vance said. "And my luck is running at cards. I want to get back to the game. And I want him to sober up. He's got to ride tomorrow."

Iggy was slicking back his hair, preening his sleeves. "I will sing the *señorita* a song," he stated. "A very beautiful song about a lover who died of a broken heart when his sweetheart died after a lingering illness."

"I can hardly wait to hear it," Della said. She eyed them both skeptically. "There's something counterfeit about this. This young man isn't as drunk as he is trying to make out. In fact, I don't think he's drunk at all. Just what are you two up to, Mr. Barret?"

"You are a suspicious person," Vance said. "I just don't want Iggy to be wandering around loose for a while. If you will let him hang around here, I'll put those three dollars on the nose of my horse tomorrow. We're going to race him again. It's all set."

"Make it ten dollars," she said. "Should we call it a

74

bribe?"

"You are a mercenary wench, aren't you?" Vance said.

"All of us have to pick up a dollar here and there wherever possible, or starve," she said.

"All right," Vance said. "Ten it is."

He left Iggy to the mercies of Della Judson, and returned to the Buffalo Palace. The Nellos and Jim Leatherwood were absent. So was Chick Nello. Vance returned to the poker game. It ran along uneventfully for an hour. Then Leatherwood returned to the place with the two Nello brothers. Each bore the look of the cat that had swallowed the canary. They began toasting each other with whisky.

Summoning Johnny Briscoe, owner of the Palace, Lige Nello produced a roll of bills and counted out three hundred dollars. Calling Vance to the bar, he made a loud ceremony of covering the wager Vance put up for the match race, placing the money in Briscoe's hands as stakesholder.

"Kiss your money goodby, tinhorn," Lige said.

Leatherwood had glanced Vance's way only once. An eyelid had drooped the merest trifle. He did not look at Vance again.

Vance returned to the game, but soon cashed in his chips. He was only a few dollars ahead. He strolled out of the gambling tent. The medicine show was closed for the night, the platform curtained with walls of frayed canvas.

Vance mounted the roan and rode to the kitchen tent at the rear, where a lantern still burned. He found Iggy entertaining Della with a ceaseless flow of rhetoric that was concerned exclusively with Iggy's exploits of romance and his bravery against odds.

"Take him away before I fall from exhaustion," she appealed to Vance as he dismounted. "He actually has

75

me almost believing all these things he talks about."

"You think I make up these amazing things?" Iggy demanded mournfully.

"I think you make them up," Della said. "But I also think you are wonderful. For, to you, life is wonderful."

She moved in and kissed Iggy on the cheek. For once, Iggy was left speechless, his eyes round with wonder. "Will you marry me, *señorita?*" he croaked. "Now! Tonight?"

Della laughed. "Thank you, Iggy. I'm flattered. But you'd never be happy with marriage. You know that. I know it."

"You show good judgment," Vance said sourly. "But he'll never be the same again. He'll be walking on golden clouds."

"I still want to know what you two are up to," she said.

"Surely you can't still believe we're up to some kind of skullduggery?" Vance demanded.

"Yes. If I ever saw signs that two rascals were fixing to do someone out of their money, or perhaps even their mortal souls, it's written on you two. What sort of skin game are you arranging?"

"*Señorita,*" Vance said, mealy-mouthed, "you desolate me by such distrust. Is there no such thing in the world as confidence in one's neighbors? We are but two poor and honest horse-racing people who—"

"Who would steal pennies from a blind man's cup if the chance came," she sniffed.

Her father appeared from the wagon, He had doffed his frock coat and was in shirt sleeves. "What's this all about, Barret?" he asked.

"I came to take Ignacio back to our wagon," Vance explained. "He's riding my horse tomorrow in a match race, and I want him to be in first-class shape."

"Match race?"

"Against that black mare Rajah beat yesterday. We expect to win. I'm ready to bet my last cent on it."

Della spoke. "A crooked race. I knew it."

"If there's anything crooked, it won't be on our part," Vance said. "We'll be as clean as new snow. You can bet your money on Rajah with a clear conscience."

"Thank you," she said.

"For the information?"

"No, for believing that even medicine-show people might have scruples. You may not believe it, but there are people worse than medicine-show fakers."

"Gamblers, for instance?" Vance asked. "Racehorse owners?"

"And spies."

"Spies?"

She had blurted out the words, but went silent as though she was wishing she could withdraw them. Her father intervened. "My daughter is tired," he said hastily. "Very tired. We've been on the platform all day. She's been upset because of that affair with the sneak thief. She is imagining there are thieves everywhere."

The girl ran to the steps of the wagon, ascended and vanished into the vehicle. "I'm sorry," Vance said. "We'll say good night, Professor."

"I must see you again—and soon," Henry Judson said. "About your horse. I beg you to call off this race tomorrow. Your animal might get hurt."

"I couldn't call it off now," Vance said.

"Why not?"

"Well, it's maybe a matter of honor now," Vance said. "Maybe your daughter would call it honor among thieves."

"I don't understand. Surely what I would pay you is

many times what you might win."

"It's no use, Professor. Have you tried to buy a good horse somewhere else? How about that black mare? Four thousand dollars would look like a gold mine to the Jones brothers after the race tomorrow, I'm sure."

Judson shook his head. "That—that is impossible. I'll talk to you again. I must prevail on you to change your mind."

Vance and Iggy rode away, mounted double on the roan. "She thinks we're spying on them," Vance said as they headed across the flat toward their camp.

"Spying? I do not understand."

"She thinks we're either Wells Fargo agents or are in cahoots with the Nellos."

"Wells Fargo? The Nellos? What are you saying?"

"I forgot that you didn't know what's going on," Vance said, and explained the situation that was working beneath the surface of the feverish camp. Iggy uttered gasps of awe and excitement as the story unfolded.

"They know the Nellos are around," Vance said. "That ought to drive some sense into their heads. Maybe they'll pull out before getting any deeper into this thing."

"That would make it much easier for us, would it not?" Iggy asked.

"For us? What are you talking about?"

"Why are we going to such trouble to win a few dollars on a horse race when we might acquire thousands upon thousands of dollars to spend?"

Vance twisted around in the saddle and gave Iggy a glare at close range. "What we would spend is the rest of our lives in a cell," he snapped. "Two men were murdered in that holdup. Somebody will swing for that.

More than that, it isn't our kind of money. We might be sharpshooters and inclined to run a high blaze or two, but only when we have to fight fire with fire. Otherwise, we've always played it on the level. You know that. Forget the Nellos. Forget the Judsons."

"You are right," Iggy sighed. "I am ashamed. I am desolated. It was my greed that got the better of me. The mention of so much money was as though the devil had appeared and was offering it to me. That sort of wealth is not for such as we are. We shall continue to eat frijoles and drink rotgut instead of caviar and champagne."

"Shut up."

"I will speak no more about the matter," Iggy said. "However, I am very, very sad, when I think of the *señorita.* She is so young, so beautiful. She will be sad also. She was falling in love with me."

"In love with *you*? Why, she never laid eyes on you until a little while ago."

"Love strikes like the bolt from the blue," Iggy said. "But now it can never be. We may never see each other again."

Vance laughed jeeringly. "Are you out of your mind? She is only after that eighty thousand dollars, and is grabbing at any straw that might help her get it, you being that straw." Then he added, "Or me."

"I cannot believe this," Iggy said. "She is not the kind to place money above affection. It is my opinion that she refrains from showing her real love for me because she knows she might spend years in the *cárcel.*"

"Just what I was saying," Vance growled. "It's the money she's after. And she thinks we're after it too."

"She did not really believe it when she cried out that we were spies," Iggy said. "I am endowed with the talent

79

for judging such things far better than you. She said that only to drive me away from her. She does not want me to get involved. It is my belief she thinks there is danger. As you said, two murders have already been committed. One life more would not matter now. It is best to keep out of this affair. I strongly advise it. I would not want to have to bury you, *amigo*, in this unfriendly country, with cornfields and turnip patches growing around your grave. Such a fate is not for you. Nor for me."

Vance said, "Be quiet." But he felt that what Iggy had said was true. Turnip patches and cornfields were not for a man like him. Such things were for these grubbers of the soil who were about to make the greatest gamble of their lives in the race for land. He and Iggy were free, independent, masters of their own destinies.

Iggy leaped from the roan and hurried ahead on foot, unable to restrain his eagerness as they neared their camp, but Vance, caught in a heavy, listless mood, only slowly dismounted and drew the rig from the roan. Their evening fire had faded to wind-fanned embers. Their canvas-tilted wagon loomed against a background of oaks and willows. Iggy rushed past the wagon to where their livestock was on night picket.

Vance heard him chuckle gleefully. He came back, rubbing his hands together in the mock sign of a miser. "It is done," he breathed. "These crooks, they fell for it. They have been there. Poor Rip Van Winkle, they must have run him very fast and hard. He is still angry. He tried to bite and kick me. Even me, his friend. He acts as though I am responsible for disturbing his rest."

"Rajah?"

"He will be able to run fast tomorrow. It will be what you call a mortal cinch. It is unfortunate that we did not see to it that we lost the race the other day. Then we

80

could ask for odds."

"That wouldn't have been honest," Vance said, grinning.

"We are the only honest persons around," Iggy said. "It is our opponents who have set the trap for themselves, and have been caught in it."

"With a little prodding from our side," Vance said. "It was Leatherwood who baited the trap, you know."

Iggy sighed. "There are times, *señor,* when I do not understand you. This should be a moment of rejoicing, not of examining one's principles."

Vance led the roan to the creek, let it nuzzle the water for a while, then picketed it on the line with the mules and the two horses. The mules were dozing, the Josephat mule resting his head on the neck of its pal, Jeremiah. They were so perfectly matched that Vance doubted that even Iggy was always certain which was which of the animals whose welfare and health were his greatest concern.

He appraised two of the horses on picket. One appeared to be the uncurried, happy-go-lucky spare mount that had been named Rip Van Winkle. The animal seemed to be content, standing hipshot, lulled by the presence of other livestock and the nearby humans. The other mount was nervous and fretting. Its two white stockings and the blaze on its forehead carried streaks of dust and dried sweat. It acted as though it had been recently hard-ridden. It bore the blanket with Rajah's name threaded on it.

Vance returned to the camp circle. *"¡Hola!"* Iggy said, beaming. "Perfect, is it not? That Leatherwood, he should be on the stage. He is one very, very good actor. I cannot wait to see the faces of these *ladróns* when our *caballo* prances to the starting line, fresh and full of run,

81

tomorrow."

"Make sure you get all the coloring off both horses and get Rip mudded and dusted up again. Poor fellow, they really gave him a workout."

"Good enough for him," Iggy said. "It is time he once again earned his grain. He is a lazy one."

Vance turned in for the night, but again he twisted sleeplessly for a long time. He was twenty-seven years old, and this was his way of life—living by his wits, gulling those who tried to hoodwink him.

The face of Della Judson kept rising before him, driving sleep farther from him. Didn't she know what she was risking? Didn't she know that even if she and her father got their hands on that Wells Fargo money, it would only leave a stain on their lives? Even if she got away with it, didn't she know that the law would never cease hounding her, waiting to pounce, waiting for the false step that would lead her to prison, or even to the gallows?

He could tell her what lay ahead. He could tell her how it was to always be watched and suspected. He could tell her about midnight raids by the law in the hope of turning up evidence, of being avoided by neighbors. He had known these things as a boy when his father and brothers had been riding long. His mother had known them too, and they had sent her to her grave before her time.

"*¡Señor!*" Iggy spoke in alarm from his bed in the wagon. "Are you ill?"

"No, of course not."

"But you moan and sigh so that you keep me awake."

"You're hearing things."

"Love is a fearful burden, is it not?"

"What in blazes are you talking about now?"

"Ah, it is the beautiful *señorita* I am thinking of. She must be sleepless also, pining for me."

"Bah! Go to sleep!"

"Is it the thought of caviar and the champagne that is keeping you awake, *mi patrón?*"

Vance did not answer that. He lay a long time, rigid, trying to think clearly. And failing. Was it his concern for Della Judson that swayed him? Or was Iggy right? Was it the temptation of that eighty thousand dollars that kept tantalizing him, driving sleep from him?

CHAPTER 7

VANCE RODE TO THE RACETRACK EARLY IN THE AFTER-noon to watch the running of the opening events of the day.

The Nello brothers, Lige and Art, were already present, and evidently had been awaiting his arrival, for they were quick to place themselves in his path. "Since you figure your blazeface is so good, fella," Art Nello said, "maybe you'd like to try to sweeten the pot a little. We've raised a hundred dollars more that says our black mare kicks dust on the face of your gelding today."

They were grinning, trying to badger him into rashness. They were men who felt they were sitting back of four aces.

"I'm out of ready cash," Vance said, "and no time to send for more. But just to make it interesting, let's make it winner take all. I'll put up my horse against your horse."

That brought them up short. They eyed Vance with sudden suspicion. Under the rules of the match race, the stake that had been put up with Johnny Briscoe went to the winner, even if the other horse failed to go to the post. The Nellos had rather expected that Vance would have realized that his horse had been tampered with, and would not show up at all. Now a doubt entered their mind that somewhere along the line there was a flaw, and that this wasn't such a sure thing, after all.

"Why, man, that mare is worth two animals like that chestnut crossbred o' yours, an' will prove it," Lige said uneasily.

"In that case, you ought to jump at the chance to win my horse," Vance said. "Take it, or leave it. Winner take all, purse and horses."

The Nellos dropped the matter and moved away. Later, Vance saw them talking earnestly with Chick Nello. Scattering, the three brothers moved among the bystanders. Vance was amused. He knew who they were looking for—Jim Leatherwood. But the tall man was nowhere to be found. He had been the buddy and pal of the Nellos the previous day. Now he had wisely dropped out of sight.

When time for the match race approached, Vance rode to the camp and helped Iggy saddle the chestnut runner. They draped a blanket over the animal, and Iggy rode double with Vance as they returned to the course, leading their entry. They did not remove the blanket until the starter bellowed the announcement of the match race and ordered the contestants to take to the track.

All three of the Nello brothers were on hand when Vance pulled the blanket from the blazeface. They peered for a silent space of time at the chestnut, which was sleek and curried, dancing about, excited, and obviously in fine fettle. Lige and Art Nello, who were none too quick-witted, seemed merely puzzled and confused. Chick, who still kept apart from his brothers, had the bitter, fixed look of cold fury. Chick was the only one who fully realized how his brothers had been

84

outwitted.

Vance lifted Iggy into the saddle. "Just worry about the other rider and any skullduggery he might try," he said "Don't worry about anything else, such as a slug in the back. I'll speak to the Nellos, and drop a hint that anybody who pulls a gun will find himself suddenly very dead."

"*Gracias,*" Iggy said. "I will have no fear now."

He rode down the track alongside the black mare which had the Nellos' gnarled rider aboard.

Vance spoke to Lige and Art Nello. "We'll keep our hands off our guns today," he said. "I don't want my horse or my rider hit by a slug, accidentally or otherwise. Any man who fires a shot better be ready to keep on shooting, for I'll come at him throwing lead."

They did not answer, but he saw that Lige passed the word on to Chick Nello a moment later. He was sure that the Nellos, by this time, knew who he was and his reputation. He doubted if that would entirely influence Chick Nello. The man was a killer, and no doubt fast with a six-shooter. But the Nellos could hardly risk starting a gunfight at this time. Not with eighty thousand dollars waiting to be found somewhere.

The race itself was hardly a contest. The black mare stayed with Rajah for only the first fifty yards, then lost ground steadily, winding up beaten by three lengths.

Chick Nello had disappeared, but Lige Nello came blustering up to Vance, livid with fury. "You run a ringer in on us," he raged.

"In what way? Isn't that the same horse your mare ran against the other day? And was beaten?"

"Why—why—" Lige couldn't find anything to say, realizing he had already said too much.

"Never gamble on a dark horse," Vance said. "At least when you ride him in the dark, Lige. You might

85

pick the wrong horse. *¡Adiós!"*

He and Iggy led Rajah back to camp, cooled him and rubbed him down. Then Vance rode into Gone Tomorrow. He first collected his winnings from Johnny Briscoe at the Buffalo Palace.

"You look as smug as an owl in a persimmon tree," Johnny Briscoe said. "How did you work that flimflam?"

"Not with mirrors," Vance said. "You've heard of giving a man enough rope to hang himself, haven't you?"

"If I was you," Briscoe said, "I wouldn't sit in any poker games tonight—at least in my place. Particularly in my place. I don't want any blood for the swampers to have to clean up. And wherever you play or sit, I'd advise making sure you got a blank wall at your back."

"You mean I've rubbed the fur of someone the wrong way?"

"The fur of some very mean catamounts. One in particular. He calls himself Bill Sands. I happen to know that ain't his real name, which I don't care to mention. In this business I've learned to keep my mouth shut. What I do know is that the one whose fur really got rubbed is *muy malo.* Very bad. A killer, right from the chunk. I also happen to know he's in cahoots with them two that pretend to own the black mare. Them two are small bore, but the one I'm talking about is hard formation. He don't like to be laughed at, like they're laughin' at his brothers all over this camp right now. Everybody knows that you run that high blaze on the ones that was tryin' to thimblerig you."

"Thanks for the information," Vance said. He drew a gold piece from the money Briscoe had handed over. "Could I ask another favor?" he said. "Would you see to it that this gets to Princess Delilah? She asked me to put

86

up a bet on my horse. I also owe her the price of a meal."

"The fortuneteller? I guess she didn't need a crystal ball to know that she was going to win."

"Wrong. On her part, at least, it was an honest bet. See to it that she gets what I owe her."

Full darkness had come by the time he returned to camp. Jim Leatherwood and Iggy were heel-squatted around the fire, where Iggy was cooking a meal. Leatherwood had brought a bottle, and he and Iggy had already sampled its contents. They pocketed their shares of the money Vance handed over to them. It was a three-way split. Leatherwood got out another tin cup, sloshed whisky into it, and more into his own and Iggy's cups. "Here's to Rajah and Rip Van Winkle," he said, grinning, "the best pair of twins it's ever been my pleasure to know."

"Eat hearty," Vance said. "And drink hearty too, if you want to regret it in the morning. I can do the driving. Then pack up. We're pulling out."

"Pullin' out? When?"

"Tonight. As soon as we can bust camp."

"Tonight? Why, fer gosh sakes? We got money to spend, an'—"

"You can spend it in Arkansas City. Or maybe Fort Smith, if we take a notion to head in that direction."

"You mean we ain't stayin' to watch the run? A sight like that? It's goin' to be *somethin'*. It'll be a race like nobody ever saw before, nor will likely ever see again. It'd be a shame to miss it."

"I was told a few minutes ago that if I hung around here I'd likely win a piece of land without even making the run for it," Vance said. "A piece about six by three. And a chunk of metal to go with it. A bullet in my back. And you two will likely get the same."

"The Nellos?" Leatherwood asked scornfully. "Don't

tell me you've got the wind up about *them?* Not you?"

"I was told that Lige and Art don't stir up much dust, but that the older one is dangerous and on the prod. He's not taking kindly to be played for a sucker."

"Chick Nello is mean, no question," Leatherwood said. "And a born dry-gulcher. But I never knew you to raise any goose bumps just because a leppie like that got his neck bowed. You've bumped into some a lot tougher than Chick, an' never gave ground. There's something else eating you. And its name isn't Nello."

"Let's just say I'm tired of Gone Tomorrow. Also, that there's a time when a man decides it's best to run scared."

"It is my opinion," Iggy spoke, "that *el patrón is* confronted by one far more dangerous than this Chick Nello."

"You don't say?" Leatherwood exclaimed. "Now, what sort of *hombre* would that be?"

"It is possible that this fearful person wears petticoats," Iggy said.

Leatherwood glared accusingly at Vance. "A woman? You've got yourself into woman trouble? Well, that's different. That's the worst kind of misery. Maybe we better hit the trail sudden."

"Don't be ridiculous!" Vance snorted. "Iggy's been looking at the redeye too long."

"Who's this gal he's got mixed up with?" Leatherwood demanded of Iggy.

"She is a princess. A *bruja*—a witch—perhaps. She foretells the future. But, unfortunately for *el patrón,* it is myself, Ignacio Guadalupe Espinosa, she admires."

"You mean it's that medicine-show girl you're talking about? The Judson girl, what's mixed up in that train holdup?" Leatherwood turned and glared at Vance.

"You fool! If you had to get balmy about a woman, why did you have to pick *that* one? That's prison bait. Gallows bait."

"You're both drunk," Vance snapped. "Della Judson means nothing to me. And Iggy means nothing to her. He's got a crazy belief that every petticoat that looks at him can't resist him. Hand me a plate, Iggy. As soon as we eat, we're pulling out, and that's the end of it."

He ladled food from the kettle onto a plate and began giving it his entire attention. He was trying to evade the fact that Iggy had told the truth. He was running scared, and it wasn't Chick Nello or his brothers who were the cause. He wanted no more part of Della Judson and the visions of her spending her life in prison. He only wanted to forget her.

Iggy and Leatherwood, realizing that it was best not to pursue the matter, ate also, resigning themselves to going along with his decision. It had always been that way with the three of them.

"I vote for Fort Smith," Leatherwood finally said. "It's livelier there. And down at the jail near the river the hangin' business ought to become right brisk once the land rush starts. There'll be plenty o' killin's over the rights to claims. Boomers will gun down claim jumpers, claim jumpers will blast boomers in arguments over corner stakes. I've seen it durin' the rush into Sioux land up north, an' in minin' stampedes. They've got a scaffold at Smith where they can pull the trap on six or more at a time when the docket gets too crowded. Now, won't that be fun?"

"I hear that even women are sent there to be hung," Iggy said with a shudder "I do not like such things. Let us head back west, toward Santa Fe or Denver. Denver is a beautiful place in summer, where the *señoritas* have roses in their cheeks and walk so straight and proud. It is the altitude that makes them thus. But, then, there is Santa Fe, which is even higher and where the *señoritas* are even more—"

He broke off. Vance had drawn his six-shooter. One instant he had been sitting, a plate on one of the wagon boxes, a fork poised in the hand. The next moment the fork was falling to the ground, he was crouching, peering off into the darkness over the blue steel of his Colt.

"Come on in!" he spoke. "Show yourself!"

A shadow moved in the brush beyond the wagon. "It's me, Henry Judson," a voice spoke.

Judson came into the firelight, and Vance lowered his pistol. Judson wore the tall hat, frock coat and patent-leather boots of his role. He had come on foot.

"You *do* draw fast, Mr. Barret," he said hollowly. "I expected to be shot. Thank heaven, you held your fire."

"You will get punctured someday, injunin' up in the shinnery like that, Professor," Leatherwood chided. "Why didn't you come in by way of the road? We'd have sighted you sooner an' knowed who you was."

"I took a shortcut," Henry Judson said, although it was obvious that he had gone far out of his way to take advantage of cover in the timber. His eyes kept moving apprehensively toward the dark foliage in the background. "Mr. Barret, I came to talk to you—in private, if these two gentlemen don't mind."

"These two gentlemen are my partners, and anything you have to say will be heard by them," Vance said. "And it will go no farther."

"It's about your horse," Judson said. "About buying him."

"I'm afraid it's no use," Vance said.

Henry Judson lowered his voice and again glanced toward the brush. "I could offer you a considerable sum?" he said. "Say, eight thousand dollars."

Vance studied Henry Judson's face. It was a powerful face, strong-jawed, bushy-browed, intelligent. The face of an idealist, a planner, a man who dreamed big dreams. And it was also the face of a man who had seen those dreams fail, seen his ideals crumble against the battlements of life.

Leatherwood had said that Henry Judson had originally been a preacher, a man who expounded the Word and tried to save souls from the fires of hell. Apparently, somewhere along the line doubt had come, and disillusionment. Henry Judson had turned his back on his original precepts and had become a horse trader, a medicine-show faker, a gypsy. And also the father of a son who had ridden with outlaws and murderers, and who had double-crossed even his own accomplices.

The face that Vance was looking into now bore lines of anxiety and almost despair. Henry Judson's stubble of beard was gray, frosting his rugged features. His eyes were bloodshot, haggard. His hands, big, gnarled, which must have swung a reaper's scythe in the past, or held the handles of a breaking plow, were now taut and quivering.

Vance held pity for this man, and regret at his inability to help lighten his travail. "No, Professor," he said. "I'm sorry, but the horse is not for sale to you. Not at any price."

"I must have him," Judson said hoarsely. "I'll pay—anything."

"Don't do this, Judson," Vance said suddenly. He had not intended to blurt any such thing, hadn't wanted to reveal that he knew about the eighty thousand dollars. It was too late to withdraw the words. For Henry Judson

91

understood.

Instantly Judson was a different man—a man on his guard, his hackles raised, ready to defend himself against the terrors of his roving world, this world of lawlessness, of confidence men, of gunmen and killers. "What do you mean, Barret?" he demanded.

He began backing away. He believed now that Vance was an enemy, an opponent who would betray him, use him, try to get the train-robbery loot away from him.

"I've made a mistake," he said. "I misjudged you."

"You're misjudging me, right enough," Vance said. "I tell you again, for your daughter's sake as well as your own, not to go ahead with this. Money isn't worth the price you'll likely have to pay."

"My daughter was right," Judson mumbled. "She suspected you were either in with—with them, or in it for yourself. You're after it too, aren't you—the money? That's why you won't sell the horse. You want us out of the way."

"You're wrong," Vance said. "I want no part of it. And you should have the intelligence to know what's ahead for you. You know the Nellos are here, watching you. And the Wells Fargo agents too. You can't beat the both of them."

Henry Judson continued backing out of camp toward the darkness. "Damn all of you!" he said hoarsely. "Damn all human greed!"

He turned and vanished into the brush. Vance could hear him crashing through bushes, moving westward along the creek. Then the deep concussion of a six-shooter erupted in the timber. The flash was a fast wink of crimson that left with Vance the memory of willow and oak fronds outlined against the blackness. The canvas tilt of the wagon above Vance's head vibrated slightly to the explosion. The heavy echoes of the shot faded quickly in the night.

Vance's first thought was that the bullet had been intended for him. He started instinctively to dive for cover. Then he realized that he had heard the soggy sound of the slug striking flesh, and the outburst of breath driven from agonized lungs.

Six-shooter in hand, he ran, crouching, into the brush, his eyes seeking a target. He could hear the wheezing of an injured man ahead—also the footsteps of someone running. Or perhaps more than one. Then that merged with other sounds as campers along the creek aroused. Men were shouting, asking questions and moving about. It was impossible to pinpoint the direction in which the receding footfalls had been heading. He believed he heard the sound of horses, as though saddle mounts were moving away at a fast pace. That, too, faded.

He came upon Henry Judson. The medicine-show man was slumped over a clump of scrub willow as though kneeling in prayer. He had been hit in the back by a bullet, and it had sent him plunging forward. His arms had instinctively stretched out to cushion his fall. He was alive, but wheezing and unable to move.

CHAPTER 8

LEATHERWOOD AND IGGY ARRIVED. LEATHERWOOD and Vance lifted Henry Judson and carried him back to the light of the lantern and the fire. Iggy spread a tarp. They placed Judson face down, and Vance, with a knife, slit his coat, shirt and undershirt. The bullet had struck off center, damaging a shoulder blade, and had emerged near the armpit.

"Doubt if it got a lung, or he'd be showin' blood at the lips," Leatherwood said. "It's a bad one, nevertheless.

But I've seen 'em pull through from a lot worse."

Other boomers had arrived and were asking questions. "This man was bushwhacked," Vance said. He added, "Likely for his money. Did any of you see who did it? Did you see anybody running away? Or riding away?"

It was a futile question. Gone Tomorrow was a community where men lived only for survival and the chance to race for free land. Nobody spoke. Even if any had seen the assailant, the odds were that he would never tell. These people wanted no part of a coroner's hearing, or of being held as a material witness at a time like this on the eve of the run. Much less did they want to be involved in what might be a gun feud whose ramifications could run deep.

Was there a doctor in camp? Only the Army had doctors. Iggy saddled Vance's roan and headed away.

"Somebody go to the medicine-show wagon and fetch the young lady," Vance said.

"My Gawd, it's the Professor what got shot," a bystander said. "I didn't know who it was at first. Now, why would anybody try to kill him? He was only a windbag, an' didn't do anybody any harm. I'll saddle up an' fetch the princess. She told my fortune only this afternoon. Looks like she might have perdicted what was goin' to happen to the professor." The man hurried away.

Henry Judson stirred, fighting off agony. "Don't move," Vance warned. "We'll have a doctor here soon. Better to lie quiet. You've been shot, but you'll be back on your feet soon."

Judson, with convulsive energy, knocked away Vance's hands and managed to partly sit up. He fumbled at the inner breast pocket of his coat, whose tatters still clung to his arms.

He uttered a moan of despair. "They got it!" he mumbled. He sank back, weakness draining him. Vance and Leatherwood fought to stem the flow of blood from his wound, using improvised bandages that boomers and their women brought from their camps.

Della Judson arrived, riding double with the man who had left to summon her. She left the horse and ran to her father's side. "How bad?" she asked Vance.

"We're not sure," Vance said. "It's bad enough, but the bone might have deflected the bullet."

"Who shot him?"

"He was shot as he was leaving this camp. I imagine you know why he came here tonight. Whoever did it got away. There was a lot of confusion. People began running from everywhere. I'm sure there was more than one who had been waiting to ambush him. I believe I heard at least two men running through the bushes. We've sent for a doctor."

He leaned close so that only she could hear. "They seemed to have been after something he was carrying in his pocket. And they got it He was able to talk a moment ago. Whatever it was, is gone."

She gazed at him an instant, and he could see complete despair and defeat in her. Then she shook that off and took over the care of her father. Vance and Leatherwood followed her directions. An Army physician finally arrived. He was a brusque, long-nosed man in his fifties who had served through the Indian wars. Bullet wounds were routine to him.

He opened his medical bag and made a preliminary examination by the light of lanterns. He shrugged. "That slug probably drove a lot of foreign matter into the wound. Particles of clothing mainly. I can't work on him here. Can you make room in that wagon to lay him out on a stretcher, or tables? I'll need good light—more lanterns."

"Will he—will he live?" the girl whispered.

"Probably. It's too early to tell. I've seen worse. I've seen better. In cases like this it usually depends on the patient, not the doctor. Depends on how tough he is, and how much he wants to live."

Iggy and Leatherwood helped Vance hastily clear their gear from the wagon and arrange an operating table on wagon boxes covered with a blanket and sheet. The doctor worked for a time while Della Judson hovered anxiously at his side, giving what help she could.

Finally the doctor stepped back. "He's got a good chance," he said. "No lung damage, apparently. It's mainly shock and loss of blood. At his age that's no minor ailment, but he should pull through if he takes it easy. I've given him an opiate. He should sleep for hours. There's little more I can do now, nor you, except to see that he's kept absolutely quiet."

He handed Della Judson a vial. "If he awakens and is in great pain, give him a spoonful of this in a small quantity of water. I'll come by in the morning to see how he is doing."

After the doctor had left, she watched over her father for a time. He lay breathing heavily under the influence of the drug. She finally left the wagon and joined Vance and his companions at the fire. All but a few of the boomers had drifted back to their camps, and those who remained also left, somewhat disappointed. They had expected more entertainment—at least hysterics and weeping from Della Judson.

She was not taking it as stolidly as they believed.

Vance saw the way her lips were quivering. He guided her to a seat in a camp chair that Leatherwood provided, and she sank into it limply, fighting off the shattering nerve tension that threatened to go out of control.

"A little touch of spirits, Jim," Vance said to Leatherwood. "Soften it with a little water."

She managed to gulp down the stimulant. She gagged and shuddered, but it finally drove a small surge of color up from her throat into her wan cheeks. She tried to think. "Our wagon!" she exclaimed. "There's nobody to watch it!"

"Iggy," Vance said, "you and Jim hustle up there and close up the medicine show. Hook up the professor's team and fetch the whole outfit down here where we can keep an eye on it."

"That will be best," Della Judson said. "Thank you." She watched Iggy and Leatherwood ride away, then walked to the wagon and made sure her father had not moved. She returned to the fireside.

"What are you going to do now?" Vance asked. "What are you thinking?"

"Thinking?"

"It's time to quit being mysterious," Vance said. "I'm not a spy, and you must know that by this time. The last thing I want to get mixed up in is whatever you're doing. In fact, we were about to break camp and pull out when your father was shot."

"That would be a wise move," she said. "I strongly advise you to do so."

"I told you that whoever ambushed your father got what they were after," Vance said. "Isn't that about the end for you and the professor? You should pull out too."

She did not answer. "What was it they got from your

father?" he demanded. "It was a map, wasn't it?"

She gave him a measuring look and decided to continue holding him at a distance. "I don't know what you're talking about," she said.

"It was a map, wasn't it?" Vance snapped. "And the Nellos have it."

He had brought her to bay. But she still tried to brazen it out. "The Nellos?" she asked. "Who are they?"

"You know who they are," Vance said. "And so do I. And I know about that eighty thousand dollars you and your father are trying to get your hands on. They were after a map the other night when you surprised them searching your wagon. When they didn't find it, they watched your father and must have guessed that he decided to carry it himself in case they came back to the wagon. Now they've got it. And you ought to get that money out of your mind."

"I—I still don't know what you're talking about," she said weakly.

"Stop that. I'm only trying to help you. Don't you realize that you and your father are playing with dynamite? You two are greenhorns up against professionals. The Nellos are killers. At least Chick Nello is. Your luck nearly ran out tonight. Your father nearly got his ticket to a grave for playing with fire. He might still fail to pull through. Don't you realize that you might be next on the list if you keep going ahead with this?"

She abandoned all pretense at innocence. "How do you know these things?" she demanded. "You—you must be one of them."

"One of the Nellos? Don't be a fool."

"How else could you know?"

"Jim Leatherwood has friends who know everything.

He also knew your father years ago back at Santa Fe. He also knew the Nellos. Everybody knows about the robbery, and how your brother double-crossed the Nellos and got away with the money."

"You're wrong!" she began. "He was—" She broke off.

"Your brother is dead, and that money is cached somewhere out in the Territory, isn't it," Vance went on relentlessly. "That's what you and your father are after."

"Where did you get such wild notions," she said icily. "Our names happen to be Judson, but the world is full of Judsons. What if I told you I never had a brother?"

"You haven't any now. He's dead."

"You're trying to pry information out of me. You're wasting your time, Mr. Barret."

"Is that why you offered so much money for my racehorse?"

When she did not answer that, he went on. "I tell you again, I'm not interested in this sort of money. And you better forget it too. Don't you know that Wells Fargo agents are here? They're watching the Nellos, and it's a sure bet they know who you and your father are, and what you're here for, and are keeping cases on you also. They expect one or the other of you to lead them to that money, then they'll swoop down on you. That's the only reason they haven't moved in on the Nellos already."

"You—you're only trying to frighten me."

"That's right," Vance said. "And you have good reason to be scared. You're gambling for big stakes. Your life in prison, or maybe a life of being hunted."

"Are—are you sure about—about the Wells Fargo men?" she asked shakily.

"I'm sure of only one thing," Vance said. "And that is

that, beyond a doubt, you're being watched even now."

"Now?"

"Yes, now. I'm sure that at least one of those people who rushed in here after your father was shot was an express detective. I've spotted him before. Leatherwood thinks so also. Your father probably was being trailed when he came here to try again to talk me into selling the runner, but they had to stay far enough away so that the Nellos were able to bushwhack him and get away. Don't you understand that this thing is finished, as far as you're concerned. The Nellos seem to have what they wanted. It's between them and the Wells Fargo men now. Maybe you have played in luck. Go back to where you came from, and forget all about this."

"I—I can't. I just can't."

"Blast it!" Vance exploded. "Can't I drive anything through your head? You saw what just happened to your father. It'll happen to you. They hang people for being accessory to murder. Even women. You're walking into a trap. The Wells Fargo people likely didn't want to stop the Nellos, even if they had the chance, when they shot your father. They still need *somebody to* lead them to that money."

He paused a moment, then added, "You, or the Nellos. It makes no difference to them. And it isn't entirely the money they're after. It's the guilty. Two men were killed in cold blood. One was an express messenger, the other a trainman. Both the Santa Fe Railway and the Wells Fargo people want to show that things like that are mighty unhealthy."

"My brother had no part in—in the killings," she burst out.

Vance was silent. She took that for skepticism. "Why, he wasn't much more than a boy," she went on. "He

100

wasn't even nineteen." Her voice was beginning to break. "He looked and acted older. He was a wild boy who wouldn't listen to advice. Mother died when we were very young. Father had been a preacher, but her death embittered him. He became a roamer. We lived hand-to-mouth. Father became a horse trader, a traveling salesman, a barker for honkytonks in mining camps and trail towns, a medicine-show faker. My brother grew up in that life—drifting. All he had to look to were sharpers, tricksters, wanderers like Father. He didn't know what he was getting into that night the train was held up."

"Why didn't he?"

"You wouldn't believe the truth, even if I told you," she said. "You've already judged my brother. So have other people. Who are they to say that he is guilty when they don't know the truth? Who are you to say it—you a trickster in your own right, a sharper who just hoodwinked others in a crooked horserace?"

"It wasn't crooked—on our part, at least," Vance said. "But you're the person we're discussing, not me."

"How do you know so much about—about me and my brother, unless you're one of them?" she demanded.

"You mean you still think I might be in with the Nellos?"

"Or with the express company," she said.

"You don't really believe that," he said. "I'm the son of Jubal Barret—the outlaw, remember? Jim Leatherwood told me that your brother and the other fellow who doubledecked the Nellos were shot up by the Nellos so bad they both died of their wounds. You Judsons buried your brother and have never told where the grave is. Leatherwood isn't the kind to make up stories out of whole cloth. He's got sources of information that I don't know about, and don't want to

101

know about."

"What else did Leatherwood tell you about my brother?" she asked.

Vance was swayed by tides of anger and futility. He felt that he had not reached Della Judson at all. She was a stone wall, impervious to reason, to emotion. She was blinded to reason by the lure of the stolen money, blinded to the danger.

"What else is there to say?" he finally asked.

"Considerable," she said. "You say we are only concerned with lifting this cache of stolen money that you assume is somewhere down in The Nations. Just how would we know about it, and just how would we know where it is?"

Vance shrugged. "That, I wouldn't know. But you must have had information, and the Nellos are sure you have. What about this map they took from your father?"

"Map? Who said there was a map?"

"Look," Vance said helplessly, "I've been trying to drive some common sense into you. But—"

"Why?"

That was an unfair question. It drove him off balance for a moment. "Why? Because—well, just because. But I'm through with all this. All I can do is wish you luck. You're going to need it."

"That sounds as though you're saying goodby."

"As soon as possible. As soon as you are able to move your father somewhere where he can be well taken care of. That might be tomorrow, I hope."

"You still are against making the run?"

"I've said that before. I'm not interested in winning a beanfield."

"In that case, our offer for your runner should interest you."

102

"So, we're back to that. The answer is still no."

"Eight thousand dollars," she said. "That would be a tidy sum for a gambler, a man who has to play close to the vest in poker games, and run ringers in horse races to earn a living."

"I might be able to pick that up without having to sell my horse," Vance said. "Isn't eight thousand about what Wells Fargo would pay for getting that money back and capture of the holdup men?"

He added, "Why should I take eight thousand when I could go for the whole pot? The whole eighty thousand?"

"I thought so," she said drearily. "Now we're getting down to the truth."

"I don't want eight or eighty," Vance said. "Let's drop the discussion. I was only trying to see how far you would go. You have your limits also, don't you? After all, seventy-two thousand would be a pretty tidy stake for a medicine-show faker and a palm reader, wouldn't it?"

"How do I know it wasn't you who shot my father tonight and took that map?" she asked abruptly.

Vance glared at her. "Let's hear that again."

"How do I know that all this high-and-mighty talk about the Nellos and the Wells Fargo agents was only to throw me off, and that the reason you won't sell your horse is that you intend to make the run yourself, but not for a beanfield? Is that the real truth?"

"That's something you'll never know," Vance said grimly.

He started to walk away. She caught him by the arm, halting him. "You must listen to me!" she said, and was sobbing. "You must. If it's the money, we'll pay you anything—anything you want. Name your price."

"Wells Fargo money?" Vance asked.

"You can have it all, every dollar. The whole eighty thousand dollars."

"For your own sake, if nothing else," Vance said, "the answer is still finally and completely no."

She went wearily limp, making a gesture of defeat.

CHAPTER 9

IGGY AND LEATHERWOOD RETURNED, WITH IGGY tooling the bulky medicine-show wagon, which had the Judson team of draft animals in harness. They backed the vehicle into position near Vance's covered wagon and unharnessed.

They came into the camp circle, leading not only the saddle stock and mules, but the Judson harness animals, and formed a stable line by stretching a rope from the wagons and tethering the stock to it on short halter ropes.

"Isn't this being a little cozy?" Vance asked, dragging his bedroll to a safer distance. "I don't usually cotton to being stepped on by a horse while I sleep."

"Better to be stepped on by a hawss than to have no hawss at all," Leatherwood said. "Anythin' on four laigs that can run is beginnin' to be worth its weight in gold. Lots of horses are bein' stole. Mules too. Folks in Gone Tomorrow are gettin' edgy, what with only two days to go before the rush. There was another shootin' in town a while ago. The third killin' today. The soldiers have winged half a dozen fellers tryin' to sooner in. They shoot on sight if anybody as much as puts a toe across the deadline. Marshal Ben Wheat had to buffalo a couple of sodbusters with the barrel of his gun when he tried to arrest them for bein' drunk an' disorderly. A mob tried to take 'em away from the marshal, but the Law Committee moved in to back up the marshal."

"Law Committee?"

"Vigilantes, in other words. Gone Tomorrow has about run out of organized law an' order, so folks who don't believe in mob rule have had to take over. Some necks are goin' to be stretched before another sunup. I've seen it happen in other boom towns. Lucky that Gone Tomorrow has only a short time to live, or there'd shore be hell to pay."

"The Nellos?"

"They're still around, but layin' low. At least I spotted Chick, an' I reckon the other two are still around. Chick saw me. I thought he'd come after me because of that deadfall I prodded him and his brothers into, but he acted like he didn't know me. He don't want to make any moves that might bring the Committee down on him. Not right now with bigger fish to fry."

Della Judson had been listening. Vance looked at her. "One or the other, or both Lige and Art Nello, are probably hanging around here, keeping tabs on you," he said.

He saw her shudder a little. She moved to the covered wagon and looked in at her father. "I better sleep in your wagon tonight, Mr. Barret, so I can be handy in case he needs anything," she said. "You men can use our wagon. You'll find the cots fairly comfortable."

"Thanks," Vance said. "I wish I could say the same about our accommodations. Iggy thinks a cornshuck mattress is the height of luxury. But at least no horse will step on you."

She moved to the medicine-show wagon, entered it, and reappeared presently with a handbag and an armful of bedding. Iggy hastened to help her with the burden, which they carried to the smaller vehicle.

"Thank you, Ignacio," she said. "And good night to all."

Vance started to frame a question, but she vanished into the wagon, dropping the canvas that served as a curtain at the bow.

Iggy joined Leatherwood at the fire, and they began a game that was interminable with them, pitching two-bit pieces over a ten-foot course, with empty tin cups as the targets. Vance waited for them to speak, but they let him hang and rattle.

Finally, he said, "What do you think?"

"'Bout what?" Leatherwood asked, and sent a coin landing with a plunk in a tin cup, accepting another coin as his winnings, which Iggy tossed to him.

"The Nellos have got the map or whatever they were after," Vance said. "They've got a fast horse in that black mare. It looks like all they have to do is pick up the marbles."

"And so?"

"Rajah has taken the measure of that mare twice," Vance said. "He'd do even better over a long stretch."

He again waited for them to speak. But they again let him dangle. "All right!" he gritted. "You know what I'm getting around to. Should we sell Rajah to the Judsons? The price is something we'd never dream of. Eight thousand dollars. Or even eighty thousand, if we pressed for it."

"We could do very much with either sum," Iggy sighed. "There is a silver-mounted saddle in a store in Taos that I would give very, very much to possess. I could buy a California sorrel with a long, cream-colored tail and a beautiful mane and ride into Santa Fe in such a manner that the *señoritas* would swoon by the dozen, and maybe by the scores."

"Never trust a woman where money's concerned,"

Leatherwood argued. "'Specially a good looker like this one. You'd never see any part of the eight thousand, let alone the eighty, or our horse again, if you fell for this."

"You overlook one item," Vance said. "We've got her father."

"Maybe she figures he's goin' to cash in anyway."

Vance fought back the urge to defend Della Judson against the old outlaw's callous estimate. Leatherwood might be right.

"Even so, it is a very nice sum to think about," Iggy said. "I could be tempted."

"And by a lot less!" Leatherwood said. "That's my two bits you just palmed. It was in the cup, which means it still belongs to me."

Unabashed, Iggy relinquished the coin. "There is one little thing that causes me to oppose parting with the horse," he said. "And that is the matter of who is going to ride the *caballo* in the mad race to get to this place where the money is cached?"

Vance drew a long breath and nodded. "That's what's sticking in my craw too. She intends to make the ride. And, now that her father's been shot, there's nobody else. She'd be all alone—against the Nellos."

"And the Fargos," Leatherwood said. "They'll keep tabs on both her and the Nellos. They'll go in on the run, you can bet on that."

Vance watched a man on foot drift past the camp in the shadows—just as he had watched men drift past the kitchen of the medicine show several times. The man was Art Nello.

"Now, why would the Nellos also continue to keep watch on the Judsons?" he murmured. "I just saw Art amble past. They're supposed to have the map showing where the money's cached. I don't savvy."

107

"Maybe the map didn't tell them all they needed to know," Leatherwood said. "That's it! That's why the gal hasn't give up. She's still in the running. And the Nellos still have to depend on her to lead them to the place. I'll bet an old boot on it."

Vance pretended to fall asleep soon after they turned in. Instead, he lay keenly awake, his ears tuned to all sounds. He had his six-shooter close at hand. All the camps along the creek were settling down for the night. Presently there was little to hear except the stir of hooves and the occasional snuffle of livestock. An owl sounded its raucous call, lonely and hauntingly sad. The owlhoot was supposed to be the traditional signal and password employed by long riders and outlaws following the night trails. Vance wondered if his father had ever used that password. Or his brothers. He thought of the desolate graves in which they all lay in New Mexico soil, near the resting place of his mother, with ancient Wagon Mound looming in the distance as a landmark. Only Vance ever rode that way whenever the chance came. It was only he who would sit by the weathering mounds that were gradually sinking into the vastness of the terrain, where the dim trails came over the horizon from the north, and faded into the distances to the south. The great wagons had passed that way en route to Santa Fe or to Chihuahua in old Mexico. The Comanches and the Apaches had fought each other for that land, then had fought the invaders who came in the lurching, wheeled prairie schooners. Now, all of them slept there, as did the members of the Jubal Barret band of long riders.

Vance's thoughts snapped back to the present. He had heard movement in the brush beyond the wagons. Then silence. He had felt that the sight of Art Nello scouting their camp had more significance than a desire to make sure the Judsons were still present. He waited—waited. The embers of the fire had faded to a faint glow, but came alive at times, touched by the movement of the breeze. Then he heard it again—faint rustle of disturbed brush.

Cautiously, inch by inch, he slid from the blankets. Flattened on the ground, he wriggled toward the nearest wagon. Della Judson, a faint shadow, had lifted a corner of the canvas curtain and was peering out. She was in nightdress. He knew then that he had not been alone in his vigil. She also had lain awake, keening the night for danger, haunted, no doubt, by the same uneasiness that had gripped him.

Their eyes met in the dimness. She did not speak, but only watched as he slid beneath the wagon out of her sight. On this moonless night the brush was a mysterious black cavern. Stalactites, which were really drooping branches, hung from weather-weary trees. Stalagmites were stumps and spears of new growth.

But one of these was a man! Vance came upon him almost at arm's length in the blackness, so abruptly that for a moment neither moved. Then the crouching figure lifted a six-shooter and fired at point-blank range.

Vance was darting aside, and that agility saved him from death. The flash of the gun burned his cheek. He had his own pistol in his hand, but could not bring it to bear instantly, for he stumbled over some root or rock. He managed to recover and plunge forward.

His shoulder drove into the man, sending him back. The man's gun roared again, but he too was falling, and the bullet went upward. Vance could have killed him then, but he refrained. The thought was in his mind that this might be a Wells Fargo agent.

He drove his left fist, stiff-muscled, in a clubbing

swing that struck the extended gun arm of his opponent. The blow knocked the weapon from the man's grasp. Vance punched the bore of his pistol savagely into the other's face, and drove a left fist to the stomach. The fight went out of his quarry along with a wheezing gush of breath from his lungs.

The man still had the strength to rise and run. Vance dove, trying to tackle him, but missed. He plunged on his face and by the time he could get to his feet his quarry was crashing away through the brush, and the direction was difficult to determine in the darkness.

Vance returned to the wagon. Iggy and Leatherwood were awake, armed. Della Judson still crouched at the wagon curtain.

"Who—?" Leatherwood asked.

"I'm not sure who it was," Vance said. "But my guess is it was Lige or Art Nello."

"Are you hurt?" Della Judson asked.

"No, only a hair singe. I don't think the other fellow was hurt bad either."

"Are you sure it was a Nello?" she asked.

"Who else could it have been? I could have killed him, but the thought struck me that it might have been a Wells—a sneak thief."

The shooting had again aroused the neighboring camps. A shrill-voiced woman began screeching, "Git the shuriff! Git the shuriff! It's high time we had some pertection from the law in this here place, ag'in these horse thieves an' murderers."

But none came to their camp to delve deeper into the matter. This second gunplay at this point might indicate that a feud was developing, of which the boomers wanted no part.

Leatherwood doused the embers of the fire. Vance

brought the mattresses from the pallets in the medicine-show wagon and used them to form breastworks around the cots on which the Judsons lay in his wagon. He and Leatherwood and Iggy moved their own beds into protection beneath the wagons. Finally, they turned in and got some sleep.

In the morning, Vance and Leatherwood searched the area, peering at the trampled grass and broken brush. Leatherwood picked up an object. It was a brass button, which had the head of a buffalo embossed on its surface.

"It was Art," he said. "He wore a saddle jacket with this kind of buttons. There are plenty of jackets like that around, of course, for you can buy them in any racket store, but we can bet our bottom dollar that Art's jacket is shy a button this morning."

"I remember getting a handhold on his coat when I tried to stop him," Vance said. "But he tore free."

They trailed the footprints through the brush for a distance and came to a point where three horses had been tethered. Other prints of boot heels showed that two more men had joined Art Nello there, then had mounted and headed away across the flats toward the heart of Gone Tomorrow.

"All three of them," Vance commented. "They really meant business."

"That ought to teach you not to go crawlin' in the brush after dark," Leatherwood said. "You was lucky. You might have had all three of them up against you."

"Maybe it was the best luck we all have had that I went out there and bumped into Art first."

Leatherwood eyed him, then gazed toward their camp, where Della was helping Iggy at the cookstove, preparing breakfast. "Her? They came to get her and finish her father?"

"Remember what you said about the Nellos still might not know just how to find what they're after?" Vance said. "If so, the girl is the only one who can lead them to it. They'd hardly want to kill her—now, would they? At least not until they get what they want."

Leatherwood drew a long sigh. "We *were* lucky you were awake. It was us, wasn't it?"

"They could have knifed all three of us in our sleep," Vance said.

"Then tried to make the princess talk?"

"Possibly, though I doubt if they believed they could get away with that. They might have tried to gag her and get her away where they could torture her. In any event, they don't know just where we three stand. They probably decided to try to get us out of the way."

"They couldn't be hung any higher for two or three more killings," Leatherwood said.

They returned to the wagons. Della had gone to her wardrobe again and was wearing a sunbonnet, a cotton dress and the gingham apron. There were dark shadows under her eyes. Her mouth had the pinched look of severe strain. It was obvious she had slept little, if at all.

"Your father?" Vance asked.

"I don't know," she said. "It's too soon to tell. He's awake and in considerable pain. He won't let me give him the drug the doctor left. He doesn't believe in drugs."

It was nearly noon before the Army doctor kept his promise to return. He was noncommittal after he had examined Henry Judson. "At least he's no worse," he told Della Judson. "His heart seems fairly strong, and that's a big point in his favor. By nightfall, or by tomorrow, there might be a change one way or another. I believe it will be for the better."

Not long after the doctor left, Marshal Ben Wheat

112

drove up, tooling a one-horse buggy. He was accompanied by a gun-packing man who had a deputy's badge pinned to his vest.

The marshal was also well-armed. The muzzles of a brace of six-shooters poked from open-toed holsters beneath the skirts of his coat. He limped a trifle, evidently a souvenir of his encounter the previous day with the mob from which he had been saved by the arrival of the vigilantes.

He lifted his hat to Della. "Mornin', Miss Fortune," he said gruffly. "I hear there was a couple of shootin's around this camp last night. I understand that Professor Fortune was hit an' is in bad shape."

Vance answered. "Somebody shot the professor early in the evening as he was leaving this camp. He's in the wagon. The doctor just left. He might, or might not, pull through."

"You know who done it?"

"No. Whoever it was, escaped in the darkness."

"Then there was more gunplay later on, so I hear?"

"I heard somebody sneaking around in the brush after we had turned in for the night. He took a couple of shots at me, but missed. He got away also. It likely was the same man."

"What was he after?"

"Anything he could steal, I suppose," Vance said.

"Why wasn't things like that reported to me?" Wheat growled. "It's my job, investigatin' crimes."

Jim Leatherwood spoke. "We figured you had your hands full, Marshal, what with mobs runnin' loose, an' Law Committees havin' to bail you out of trouble."

Wheat glared at Leatherwood. "Don't think for a minute that I don't know who you are, an' who you rode with in the past, Leatherwood," he said. "What part did you have in this?"

"Me?" Leatherwood exclaimed. "I hid under the wagon. I stay as far away from trouble as humanly possible, 'specially when bullets are flying."

Wheat smiled dryly. "And I bet you say your prayers every night and go to church on Sunday." He turned and looked Vance and Iggy over from head to foot. "I ought to put all three of you in the stockade," he said. "You stir up enough trouble by yourself, Barret, without hooking up with these two."

He turned to Della. "I advise you, young lady, to find better company. Good day."

To their surprise, he climbed back into the buggy, took over the reins and drove off. Vance decided that he had been prodded into making some sort of a display of enforcing the law by neighboring campers like the woman who had screamed for the "shuriff" the previous night. Wheat had been very careful not to insist on the details, and had been all too anxious to end the interview.

Della Judson moved aimlessly about the camp, obviously torn emotionally. In addition to her father being on what might be his deathbed, there was the fact that the deadline for the race for land was looming closer with each minute. Gone Tomorrow's sands of life were ebbing away rapidly now.

The run would start at noon on April 22. This was now April 20. Already some of the camps along the creek were being broken by boomers who were moving close to the deadline the cavalry had marked out across the prairie. Leatherwood, riding into the heart of the camp during the afternoon, reported that some of the gambling traps and saloons were being dismantled and loaded on wagons in preparation for following the run.

"Even the Buffalo Palace is gittin' ready to pack," he

said. "An' listen to this—Johnny Briscoe himself is goin' to make the run. He's got himself a big gray saddle horse with a paunch as big as a barrel that Johnny says kin run all week and Sunday too. Johnny is out to ketch himself a lot in one of them new towns that will spring up, an' wants to open up a permanent establishment. This land run is goin' to be one hell-raisin', gully-washin' ground-stamper, if you hear me. They say more'n ten thousand people are strung out all along the line for miles each way, ready for the run in anythin' that'll move on laigs or wheels. They say there's one feller that aims to ride saddle on a milk cow."

Della Judson spoke. "How about the cavalry?"

Leatherwood eyed her speculatively. "If anybody's got a mind to try to sooner in, they better forgit it," he said. "More cavalry has been sent in. The line is closed tighter'n a scalp-hunter's bowstring. Three fellers was shot today tryin' to belly in. They even say one was a woman, dressed like a man."

She said nothing. She knew that he had elaborated on the information as a warning to her. Vance studied her, wondering if she had something in mind, something reckless. He could see that she felt that her burden had grown heavier. Her responsibilities were pressing in on her now that she did not have her father to make the decisions.

Part of her burden was eased before the day ended. Late that afternoon Vance was sitting, watching Iggy and Leatherwood at their endless game of pitching coins. All wore their pistols belted at their sides and had rifles standing ready and loaded. The horses were held close at hand on short ropes, and the two wagons had been moved so that they offered a bulwark against the creek brush, with tarps strung on ropes to further

115

enclose the camp and give additional protection.

Della appeared from the covered wagon, where she had gone to be with her father. Her face was suddenly radiant, the brightness driving away the shadows, bringing a return of her winsome beauty. "Father's better!" she exclaimed joyfully. "Much better! I'm sure of it! Come and see!"

They all crowded to the step into the wagon. Vance mounted into the interior. Henry Judson lay on the pallet. He was obviously still in pain, but it was also plain that the issue had been decided and that he would live.

He was becoming aware of his unfamiliar surroundings. He peered with weak, puzzled eyes at his daughter, then at Vance. "You're in Mr. Barret's wagon," Della explained. "You were shot. You're going to be all right."

"Shot?" Judson mumbled. "Who—why—?"

Vance halted him. "Better not try to talk now, Professor. It's all over and everything's all right. Your daughter will tell you all about it later. Your best bet is to take it easy right now."

He returned to the pitch game. He was awaiting Della's decision. He felt that he already knew what it would be, for he was growing more and more aware of her strength and determination.

He soon had his answer. And it was the one he had anticipated and hoped he would not have to face. After the evening meal was finished, Della indicated that she wanted to speak to him alone. He joined her in the shadows near the medicine-show wagon.

"I've never begged for anything in my life," she said. "I'm begging now."

"The horse? You still—?"

"Yes. It's not a matter of money It's something far

116

more important to me." She paused, looking at him with eyes dark with a fierce play of emotion. "It's for someone—someone I love."

There was silence for a space. Vance was suddenly empty of all thought, of all desire to talk or do anything. He had been right in one thing, at least. It wasn't the money after all that was driving her. It was something greater than that—a man. Another man.

"I don't understand," he finally said tiredly.

"I—I can't explain. But it's a matter of life and death. You will have to believe that, for I can't tell you anything more. I'll pay for the horse. I'll get the money, somehow. It will take time, maybe years, but you'll be paid. I must have your horse now—tonight."

"Tonight? You mean you're going to try to sooner in—alone?"

"Yes," she said.

"Can't I make you see that it's too dangerous," he said angrily. "You *must* have heard what Jim Leatherwood just said. The deadline is closed—tight. It isn't only the soldiers you'd have to contend with. It's the boomers themselves. They're strung out along the line for miles. They'd all like to sooner in themselves, so as to get their pick of the claims, but as long as it's too big a chance to take, they're not going to let anyone else get the jump on them if they can prevent it. They'll turn you over to the cavalry. You'll be stockaded. And you might even be shot trying to cross the line. The troops have orders to shoot on sight."

She suddenly made a gesture of surrender. "I'm afraid you're right," she said. "I'm being foolish."

Vance eyed her suspiciously, surprised by her sudden change of heart. He decided that she was sincere. "That's better," he said. "Forget the whole thing. You'll live longer and be happier."

He added, "Could I make the run for you? And help this—this person."

"No—no!" she exclaimed. "I couldn't—It's impossible."

"Why, impossible?"

"I could never let you become—It's impossible. You don't understand."

She turned and ran to the wagon in which her father lay, mounted to the interior and dropped the curtain.

Vance rejoined Iggy and Leatherwood. He sat for a time heavy-spirited, still empty. Somehow all the ground had been swept away from beneath his feet. So it was a man who was responsible for the desperation he had seen in her. A man with whom she was in love.

"At least she's smart enough to know when not to bet against the odds," he finally told his companions. "She's given up the idea of making the run. I told her what might happen to her."

"It is a wise man indeed who can give advice to a *muchacha*," Iggy said. "Or a fool."

Iggy left the circle to bring the horses in for the night. "What's eating him?" Vance asked Leatherwood. "Was it me he was calling a fool? Talking that girl out of it was the only sensible thing to do."

"Who said there was anythin' sensible about this whole thing, or about us gettin' mixed up in it?" Leatherwood growled. "As I remember it, we was supposed to be on our way to Arkansas City or to Dodge or Fort Smith by this time with that race money jinglin' in our pokes, an' beef an' taters in the cookpot instead of beans."

"Beef and 'taters!" Vance exploded. "Is that the only thing we've got to look forward to in life?"

"Now, what'n blazes is eatin' you?" Leatherwood

118

demanded. "You got an all-gone look about you. Sorta like a feller I saw once that was knocked down by a spent bullet."

Della appeared, went to the medicine-show wagon, where Vance could hear her rummaging about for a time. She presently reappeared, carrying a bundle of garments. The men's small shaving mirror was hanging to a wagon tire, and with a woman's instinct she was drawn to it to inspect her hair, sigh, and try to arrange loose strands.

Then she said, "Good night, all," and entered the smaller wagon.

Vance sat, arms clasped around his knees by the fire, looking unseeingly into the flames. Leatherwood had said there had been only five men in on the holdup—the three Nellos, young Frank Judson and another young wilding, both of whom had been shot by the Nellos. Evidently, there had been another person, a man, and he was down there in the Territory, with the stolen money, awaiting Della Judson.

CHAPTER 10

IGGY WAS SLOW BRINGING IN THE LIVESTOCK. FULL darkness had come by the time he brought the last of the horses in and tethered them to the stable line. He had blanketed both the blazeface gelding and Rip Van Winkle, an unusual exertion, for the night was mild— particularly in Rip Van Winkle's case. Rip Van Winkle usually was not pampered

Vance brought pails of water from the creek and doused the embers of the fire. "No use making targets of ourselves," he said. "If we can last it out tonight without

119

being picked off, we're home safe. Tomorrow we'll move up to the deadline. By that time the professor ought to be stronger. There'll be safety in numbers at the line, we hope."

Iggy and Leatherwood were stricken motionless for a space. They stared disbelievingly at him, tin cups of coffee poised in their hands.

"What was that you just said?" Leatherwood asked.

"About what?"

"About movin' up to the deadline tomorrow."

Vance lifted the chimney on the lantern and blew out the flame, leaving them in darkness, relieved only by the distant reflection of other campfires. "Anything wrong with that?" he demanded crisply.

"You ain't thinkin' of makin' the run, are you?"

"Why not?" Vance asked.

"Why not? You mean you got the gall to stand there an' ask why not? Jehosephat! After all you've said! You mean you aim to race the rubes an' hayshakers—for a danged *farm?* You? You raisin' carrots an' other such rabbit fodder? Bringin' up crops fer grasshoppers? What about Arkansas City? An' Fort Smith? An—"

"They can wait, can't they?" Vance snarled. "I didn't say I was going to turn into a sodbuster, did I? Can't a man want to see the excitement without you two jumping to conclusions? You, yourself, said it would be quite a sight, Jim."

"It is the *bruja,* the witch," Iggy said. "She cast the spell on him."

"Go to bed," Vance growled

He drank more coffee in the darkness. So did Iggy and Leatherwood. To Vance the coffee tasted as flat and acrid as the stale smoke from the drowned embers of the fire. Vance could not shake off the slackness of mind

120

and body. He had reached a turning point in his life. He knew that. The past was dead with him. But he had no vision of any future.

Leatherwood mumbled a good night and moved to his bed, which he had made beneath the medicine-show wagon. Iggy, who preferred a roof over his head, climbed into the medicine-show wagon to turn in for the night.

Vance finally dragged his tarp and bedding into a position where any intruder would have to step over him to reach the steps of the wagon where Henry Judson and his daughter were quartered.

For the first time in several nights he fell into deep sleep almost instantly. He came out of it slowly, sluggishly. Stars were dim through the misty spring night, and an old moon was adrift in the sky. He could hear both Iggy and Leatherwood breathing heavily. Something in that sound sent a warning through him. He suddenly knew the truth. He and the other two men had been drugged. He remembered the vial the Army doctor had left with Della Judson.

He dragged himself to his feet. One of the horses was gone from the stable line. It was Rajah, the chestnut runner, that was missing.

"Della!" Vance called. "Della!"

There was no answer. He found his matches and lighted one. He pushed aside the canvas and looked inside the covered wagon. The pallet on which Della slept was empty.

Henry Judson was awake. He said, "She wouldn't listen to me, Barret. I've spent the time since she left praying that nothing would happen to her."

"Praying? You?"

"Even I pray where my children are concerned."

121

"How long has she been gone?"

"Not too long, but long enough so that you'd never overtake her, even if you knew which direction she took."

Vance shook Leatherwood and Iggy awake. "That girl softsoaped me into believing she had listened to my advice," he raged. "Then she doped us, stole Rajah, and is trying to run the deadline."

Iggy groaned and clasped arms around an aching head. "Even though she is a *bruja,* she will not get far tonight," he said. "I have seen to that."

"What do you mean?"

"If you will look closer, *mi patrón,* you will observe that it is not the fine *caballo,* Rajah, that is missing. It is that loafer Rip Van Winkle, that she led away after she was sure her witch's potion had taken effect on us. It was in the coffee, of course. I must admit that even I did not suspect she would do such a dastardly thing. I had intended to lie awake and catch her red-handed."

"You ran a ringer in on her?" Vance asked hoarsely.

"I was too shrewd for this pretty *muchacha.* I had some coloring left over, so before I brought the *caballos* in last night, I did a little work on them. I changed the white feet and the forehead streak from one to the other. I also changed Rajah's blanket. It was my belief that the *señorita* acted too docile when she agreed that you were right, *señor.* It was my belief that she intended to do exactly what she did—which was to become a horse thief."

"You fool! You know that Rip hates women riders. He'll pile her, and she'll likely be killed."

"As I told you, I expected to remain awake and catch her in the act," Iggy said. "How did I know that she was such a clever, designing female as to try to poison us?"

122

"She's likely lying out there with a broken neck," Vance groaned. "You know that horse will only wait his chance, then try to throw her over the moon."

He raced to the covered wagon. "Why didn't you stop her?" he demanded of Henry Judson.

"I tried," Judson said. "But she has a mind of her own. And please keep your voice down. *They* might be listening."

"The chances are that *they've* followed her and have got her. She'll be caught anyway if she gets as far as the deadline. If you do any more praying, pray that it's the soldiers who get her."

"She might have made it through. Surely, that horse can't be as dangerous as you seem to think. She's a good horsewoman."

"Rip Van Winkle is in a class by himself," Vance said. "He's lazy, but as tricky as they come. He's got a grudge against the world, and against women especially. He must have been worked over by some person wearing skirts when he was a colt. He might travel a mile or so, waiting until she's off guard, then go to pieces."

"If anything happens to her, I'll hold that young fool who changed horses to account," Henry Judson vowed.

Iggy spoke indignantly. "*Señor*, I am insulted. When you are able to face me, I challenge you to—"

"Shut up!" Vance snapped. "Judson, have you any idea about where she might try to run the line, and—?"

He quit talking. A dilapidated figure had emerged out of the darkness, limping into the camp circle, leading a horse on which the saddle was askew. The arrival was Della. She was wearing the jeans and denim jacket and masculine shirt in which she had disguised herself the day she had watched the races. These garments were caked with mud and dust, and the wide-brimmed hat she had been wearing hung crookedly down her back by the chinstrap.

As the men stared, she limped to Iggy and slapped him resoundingly. "Blast your scheming hide!" she wept. "I ought to horsewhip you! And shoot that damned horse."

She dropped the reins by which she had been leading Rip Van Winkle, and headed toward the covered wagon. She was near collapse. Vance moved in and lifted her off her feet. "Get some cold water, Iggy," he said. "She acts like she might have a sprained ankle."

"I suggest," Iggy said, "that you shoot her, *señor*. All she has brought us is trouble. At least we will still have Rip Van Winkle with us. He is sound, and much more valuable."

Vance placed the girl on a camp stool and lighted a lantern, ignoring the chance of a shot from the brush. He pulled off one of her boots. The ankle was slightly swollen, but the cold water Iggy brought reduced the injury, which was no more than a slight sprain.

"Did you get hurt anyplace else?" Leatherwood asked.

"Nothing that I care to discuss here and now," she sighed.

"What happened?" Vance asked.

"What do you suppose happened? You know very well what happened. That cursed horse let me ride him for a mile or so. Just when I thought he was as meek as milk, he swallowed his head, fishtailed, humped his back, and threw me into the mud along the creek. Then he just stood there as though he was enjoying it."

"Good!"

"How can you say that? What's good about it?"

"You're still alive, aren't you? And no credit to you. Instead of slapping Iggy, you ought to be kissing him. He likely saved you from being caught by the Nellos, or spending a week in the stockade."

"I must state at this point that I do not wish to be kissed by this one," Iggy spoke. "I prefer prettier ones, with more of the figure."

"That's a rude thing to say," Della sobbed.

"Iggy favors the plump ones," Leatherwood said. "He likes an armful."

They could see that she was shaking and near hysteria. They were trying to divert her, steady her. But they failed. She buried her face in her hands. "What can I do now?" she sobbed.

"You can get into bed and get some sleep," Vance said.

"Sleep? Do you think I can sleep, thinking about—about—well, just thinking?"

"Maybe you've got some of that dope you put in our coffee," Leatherwood said. "I can guarantee it'll make you forget your troubles in a hurry."

"I used it all," she sobbed.

The flash of powder flame lighted the brush beyond the camp. Vance felt a powerful force grip his arm. He was whirled violently around, and pitched backward over a wagon box. He landed flat on his back with an impact that drove the breath from him.

Two blasts came from a six-shooter close overhead. Glass shattered. Jim Leatherwood had shot out the lantern light, and had sent a bullet into the brush in search of the assailant.

In the next moment what little breath Vance had left was endangered by a weight that landed upon him. The weight was Della Judson. She wrapped her arms around him and clung to him, trying to protect him from any further bullets with her own body.

"Where are you hit?" she babbled. "Oh, it's all my

125

fault! Now they've killed you!"

Vance managed to wriggle from beneath her. He gulped down lungsful of air. He pushed her aside so that he could get to his knees and peer for a target. He crawled toward the shelter of a wagon, dragging the girl with him. He crouched there, waiting. His own pistol lay out of reach near his bed, but he knew that at least Leatherwood was armed, and Iggy also, no doubt, and that they, like himself, were hunkered down, waiting.

The camp was again black and silent. So was the brush. Nothing moved, nothing stirred. The whole world seemed breathless, poised to pounce or to flee.

Leatherwood spoke from somewhere nearby. "How bad, Vance?"

"All it did was ruin my shirt," Vance said. "It was as though somebody grabbed me and threw me bucket over tin cup. I never knew a slug could manhandle you like that without hitting anything but cloth."

"You know it now," Leatherwood said. "Your luck is still running. You've missed it twice now."

There was nothing to do but wait it out. Minutes passed. More minutes. "What can we do?" Della breathed.

She was crouching so close at his side her tumbled hair brushed his cheek. "Keep hugging the ground," Vance murmured. "They're not after you. You're too valuable to them for that."

He touched her and could feel her shivering. She knew what he meant. She had been a target as easy to hit as had been Vance, but he was the one the bullet had been meant for. No doubt, Leatherwood and Iggy might have been the next targets. The Nellos—for there was little doubt but that the shot had come from a Nello weapon—still wanted to strip from the Judsons anyone who might aid them.

The chill of the night moved in. Della instinctively pressed closer against Vance's side. He could hear her teeth chattering. He left their covert for a time and brought blankets from his bed to wrap around her. After a time, he knew that the tenseness had faded from her. Presently, he realized she was asleep, still pressed close against him. Exhaustion had finally taken its toll. She made little sighing sounds as though sure, at last, of protection from the terrors of life.

But soon, even in sleep, those terrors began to plague her. She moaned, and the tenseness came back. "Sonny!" she mumbled in her sleep. "Sonny, are you all right! Wait for me! Wait. I'm trying to come to you. Are you . . . ?"

She drifted off into sleep again. One of her arms stole around him and she clung to him, once more finding peace in his presence.

Sonny! Vance remembered the wealth of devotion with which she had uttered that name. Presently he carried her to the wagon, placed her on a pallet and covered her with the quilts. She awakened, started to ask a question. "It's all right," he told her. "It looks like they've pulled out, but we'll stand watch until morning."

She slept again. Vance and Iggy and Leatherwood kept vigil through the night, spelling each other, waiting with guns ready to take care of any killer who might try another visit But the thickets remained peaceful the remainder of the night

Della and Iggy cooked the morning meal while Vance and Leatherwood watered the stock and picketed the animals on grazing. They sat with rifles and six-shooters within reach as they ate, keeping the horses in sight and scanning the brush. It was in Vance's mind that the Nellos, having failed in their attempts to get himself and his companions out of the picture, might try to see to it that the Judsons would not have the advantage of riding a fast horse—by putting bullets into some of the saddle animals, particularly the chestnut runner.

The horses would be easy targets, of course, for even a distant rifleman, but a factor greater than the watchfulness of Vance and his companions protected them now. The timber along the creek swarmed with activity. Boomers were moving about everywhere, caring for their stock. The smoke of breakfast fires rose at every hand, along with the tang of frying bacon and flapjacks.

Anyone who fired a gun would no longer have darkness as a protection. At this stage of the gamble for land, the wanton killing of a good horse would amount to a crime as heinous as stealing one, and the guilty man could hardly escape capture. There were stories that several horse thieves had already been lynched after summary wagon-gate trials by kangaroo courts.

They ate the venison and biscuits and fried potatoes that Della served, drank the coffee and downed tinned peaches.

"Your father?" Vance asked.

"Much better," she said. "Very much better."

Excitement was increasing around them. Many camps were being struck as boomers, no longer able to curb their impatience, began moving up to the deadline. Vance, gazing toward the heart of Gone Tomorrow across the flats, saw the canvas top of another establishment go down to be packed on wagons in preparation for joining the great stampede into the new country, to be set up—perhaps before another nightfall—at some townsite that would be laid out down in the vanishing Indian Nations.

With the starting gun that would turn loose the flood of land-hungry settlers less than twenty-four hours away, the strain was growing unbearable. Tempers were short and explosive. Guns were set on quick trigger, and shootings—over trivial matters, at that—were becoming commonplace.

Men—and women too—who had never owned a foot of land for themselves, never seen a farm, whose lives had been spent in sweatshops and crowded eastern cities, had come here to make the run, dreaming of living under an open, blue sky, with no neighbors at elbow length. Many were here from Europe—Italians, Germans, French, Spanish. And the Irish, the English. Many of these would be in for bitter disappointment, lacking citizenship qualification.

Many were bona fide farmers who had worked hard-scrabble land in Maine, in the Appalachians, in the California deserts, in Oregon's rain forests where vegetation was a curse. They were here gazing longingly at virgin prairie with its timbered, sweet-water streams, its deer, its wild turkey, its promise of peace and independence and plenty.

It was these things these people sought more than even the hope of winning free land. What they wanted was room—room to breathe, to work out their futures by individual expression, room to grow up free and beholden to no man.

Some would fail. They would never be farmers, no matter how rich the claims they might win. They would never be able to accommodate their habits and personalities to the whims of nature. And nature here could be as uncompromising and as brutal as anything they had known in city or tenement. This was the land of terrible cyclones. Boomers who knew this country were warning the uninitiated that their first building project should be not aboveground but beneath it— storm cellars.

Then there would be the winters when the northers came down on the country, sheeting the prairie in ice, congealing the rivers into ribbons of blue steel. There would be Arctic gales that might blow for days at a time. And there would be stretches of searing summer heat.

But then, also, there would be those long, wonderful stretches of weather when a man felt he could jump over the moon, or uproot a post-oak tree with a twist of his finger. These would be the days that would be remembered.

Some, like the cowboys, were here merely for the hell of it. They were here to watch the clumsy sodbusters get their comeuppance down there in The Nations. The range riders had no doubts about how all this would end up. Nor the Indians. All this was a nightmare, a passing hallucination that would blow away like the winds that were said to always wind up in Kansas City somewhere far to the north and east. Then this land would be theirs again. Then they would ride wild and free once more, and once more they could sit around the chuck wagons or the branding fires and tell it long about the time the boomers came in and kicked up a lot of dust—then vanished into the blue.

Some of those joining the line were keen-minded businessmen who knew that fortunes were to be made if one picked the right spot and played his cards smartly. Townsites were to be had down there, and all a man needed was to guess which would prosper and which would wither.

The sharpers were present also. Some were self-styled experts who were signing up boomers at a hundred dollars a head on the promise they would be led to choice land only a short run across the deadline. The odds were that the majority of these guides would vanish once the run began, leaving their clients to shift for themselves.

The old and young, the vigorous and the infirm, were facing the test. For all, the deadline was the mecca. Like an army bracing itself for the charge, the contestants were beginning to form a solid phalanx along the ragged furrow, turned by an ox team that stretched along the prairie, and beyond which arrest or a cavalry bullet was the penalty for soonering. Gone Tomorrow, which had been the heart of the assembly, was now losing its identity in the endless line.

"We'll stay here until later in the day at least," Vance said. "It'll be better to keep the horses away from all that excitement as long as possible. Then we'll move up to the line."

Della paused in her camp chores and looked at him questioningly, searchingly. Then she resumed her task. This was her first intimation that Vance and his companions had changed their purpose and might take part in the race for land.

This evidently brought, at first, a rush of hope to her. Then he saw the doubts return, the same doubts that always arose in her when she looked at the facts from a cold viewpoint. She was once more asking herself what might be their real purpose in this change of heart. He could see that she feared the answer.

The truth was that he hardly knew the real answer himself. He knew only that he was now in it to the hilt, along with Iggy and Leatherwood. Despite their expressed amazement at his decision, both of his companions had known that they would see this through to the finish. The Nellos had brought that about. The Nellos had drawn first blood. In Iggy and the lanky man there was no thought of turning the other cheek.

As for the money? Vance had no answer for that either. Eighty thousand dollars might be too great a temptation for any of them to resist. In spite of himself, he could feel the faster drive of his pulse at the thought of possessing that amount of cash. He kept asking himself if that might be the real reason, after all, why he was entering the race. There could be no other reward for him now that he knew about Sonny.

Leatherwood got out the small forge, bellows and anvil from the wagon and fanned fire to heat iron. He and Vance pulled the racing plates from Rajah, and the worn shoes from Pawnee, replacing them with new iron that was shaped for rough going.

The day turned warm toward noon, then cooled in the afternoon. Clouds moved in, offering the threat of rain. Men who intended to make the run in vehicles groaned, seeing the chance of bogging down in prairie mud. The clouds dissipated and the sunset promised to be clear, bringing the promise of fine weather for the run. The mood of the boomers ran up and down the scale with each phase of the weather.

"All right," Vance said, late in the afternoon. "We might as well move up. We'll take both wagons up to the line and find a place before dark. We'll keep the runner and Pawnee between the wagons, shielded as much as possible. They ought to be safe enough with so many people around, but it's best to be careful."

Della spoke, putting the question she had been holding back for hours. "Am I supposed to know what you intend to do?"

"I'll ride the blazeface in the run," Vance said. "You will ride Pawnee. Iggy and Jim can follow with the wagons. Your father is able to travel, I'm sure—at a decent pace."

He waited for her to speak. When she did not, he said, "Iggy and Jim don't know where you and I might be, of course. I'm taking it for granted your father will know and can direct them?"

Again she did not answer. "Pawnee is a good horse," Vance said impatiently. "You need not worry about that part of it. He can't run with Rajah at first, of course, but he'll stay with him over a long stretch, particularly when he's got a lightweight rider like yourself in the saddle."

"I see," she said.

"Just what do you see?"

"Does it matter?"

"I believe you think you see a man who has decided he can't pass up a chance to get rich. You believe I'm giving you a slower horse to make sure you don't get out of my sight."

"You can be right," she said.

"At least we understand each other."

"Do we?" she burst out. "I've already told you that the money is all yours. All that matters to me is that I get there first—ahead—ahead of the Nellos. Ahead of everyone."

"Speaking of the Nellos, they'll trail you, of course. They'll be watching you every minute. They're probably watching this camp right now, making sure you don't drop out of sight."

"I'll have to lose them—somehow."

"And if you don't lose them, then what? I'll answer that for you. The Nellos aren't exactly gentlemen. Your brother doubledecked them, caused them all this trouble. They'd like nothing better than to take out some of the grudge on the Judsons. They've already tried to kill your father. They could have tried to kill you instead of me and Iggy or Leatherwood, but you're valuable to

133

them, for you seem to be the only one who knows the answer to all this mystery about where the money's hidden. Do you think they'd go easy on you if they got their hands on you? They'd make you talk. And once they got their hands on the money, do you think they'd let you live to be a witness against them?"

Vance was once more up against the stone wall of her silence. He turned to his companions for help, or at least an opinion. In their expressions he saw the same bafflement and frustration. Once again he had failed to get through to the real core of the desperation that drove her.

"You must love him very much," he said.

She was startled. "What did you say?"

"This man you call Sonny," Vance said. "Does he mean so much to you that you'd risk all this?"

"I—why—I don't understand," she stammered.

"You talked about this man in your sleep the other night," Vance said. "You called him Sonny. I couldn't help overhearing."

"I see," she said breathlessly. Then, without explanation, she hurried to the wagon where her father lay and entered it.

Henry Judson had overheard the conversation. He called out from his pallet. "We'll accept your offer, Barret. You and my daughter will make the run together."

CHAPTER 11

THE GREAT MOMENT WAS AT HAND. SILENCE HAD settled all up and down the line of humanity that stretched across the prairie. The only sounds were the movement of animals and the soft humming of the breeze in the new grass.

Cavalrymen, spaced at intervals, sat facing the multitude, ready to spur their horses away to escape the avalanche that was poised and might overwhelm them. Somewhere a drunken man broke the silence by trying to sing a bawdy song. His voice faltered and faded as he realized his mistake.

Vance then became aware of a deep undertone that grew in volume. Many people were praying—praying for guidance, for survival, for success, for wealth—for all the things that humans pray for.

He was mounted on the blazeface, riding Iggy's light saddle to save weight. He had adjusted the stirrup leathers to suit his longer legs. He had his rifle lashed to the saddle. His six-shooter was tied in its holster so that it could not be easily dislodged in case of a fall, but tied so that he could bring it into use with a minimum of delay in case of need.

At his side, Della was astride on the roan. It, too, was equipped with a light saddle, a worn spare that belonged to Iggy. She wore her denim breeches and jacket and calico shirt, and had her hair concealed beneath the wide-brimmed felt hat. None of their close neighbors in line were aware that she was a girl.

And there were their neighbors. They sat stirrup-to-stirrup in a solid line of riders who had pushed the noses of their horses to the plowed furrow. Back of the horsemen loomed the vehicles—buggies, spring wagons, even sulkies. Then the heavier wagons. Hundreds of them, some with only a single team in harness, others with up to eight horses. There was no telling the number of hopefuls, for new arrivals had swarmed in like the flight of bees to blooming flowers during the past twenty-four hours.

Vance looked at his watch. Less than five minutes.

The carbines of the troopers were loaded and held at the ready to be lifted and fired in the air when the cannons boomed.

The Nellos were near at hand. Chick Nello, on a big steel-dust gelding, was only a rod or so to Vance's left in the saddle line. Farther along were Art and Lige. Art, being the smallest, was riding the fast black mare. Lige rode a bay horse that looked capable. The Nellos were making no attempt to stay in the background, taking no chance of losing sight of Della Judson in the bedlam that was about to be turned loose. The issue was now entirely out in the open. The Nellos knew there could be no doubt but that Vance and his companions knew who had tried to murder them. Vance met the eyes of Chick Nello. Milky, ruthless eyes. Chick was the one who had done the shooting from ambush. As Leatherwood had said, Chick was the killer.

Also within sight was Marshal Ben Wheat and at least two men Vance believed were Wells Fargo agents. They were well mounted also, but not everyone in line was racing for prairie land.

There were still many questions in Vance's mind that he had not yet asked Della. He was sure she knew what those questions were, but she had not volunteered any answers. The main puzzle to Vance was the map he believed the Nellos had taken from Henry Judson. Della had never admitted there was a map, but she had not denied it either, which amounted to a tacit admission of its existence. She had not explained why the Nellos were continuing this cat-and-mouse game of watching her if they really possessed directions that would lead them to the cached money.

Leatherwood and Iggy had offered many theories as to the real purpose that was driving Della Judson. Some of them were wild and far-fetched, but one was that the money wasn't down in the Territory at all, and that she was only leading the Nellos and the Wells Fargo men on a wild goose chase while an accomplice lifted the cache miles away and escaped from the country. That accomplice might go by the name of Sonny.

"One minute!"

The word was repeated along the line. The praying ceased. The silence was a weight. Then a cannon boomed in the distance. Carbine fire crackled raggedly along the line.

These sounds were drowned out in the next moment by a thunderous roar of hooves and wheels getting under way, and of men and women screeching at the top of their lungs.

Vance kneed the blazeface into its customary shotgun start. It left Della's mount a dozen lengths behind in the first hundred yards, but he took a tight grip on the animal to make it understand that this race must be paced. Looking back, he saw that Della was almost engulfed in dust and the swirling confusion of riders who were using spur and quirt on their mounts. He steadied Rajah still more until she could pull alongside. She was frightened, but riding it out gamely.

A horse went down in the roan's path. The roan leaped over animal and rider. Della managed to maintain her seat in the small saddle and hung to the roan's mane. Other horses fell over the downed animal. The last Vance saw of this spill was a tangle of hooves and bodies. Della looked back too, and then turned and looked ahead.

He let her lead the way. The wind drove a fog of dust upon them. The great mass of buggies and wagons was rolling at full speed now. The prairie behind them was a sea of bouncing, swaying vehicles and harness teams,

137

with wild-eyed drivers urging the animals along faster.

Vance squinted through the dust. He discovered that Chick Nello was almost abreast of him, stirrup-to-stirrup. Again their eyes met, and Vance read the man's intention in time to save himself. Chick had his six-shooter in hand, and he meant to put a bullet in either the blazeface or in Vance, thereby leaving the girl without protection.

Vance had no time to draw his own pistol. It was a repetition of that meeting in the brush when he had come face-to-face with an intruder. He swung his arm in a chopping blow on Chick's gun arm an instant before the man pulled the trigger. The gun roared, its sound feeble amid the din around them. Then Nello's horse went down, pitching end over end. It had been killed by the bullet.

Looking back, Vance saw that Nello had been thrown clear. He was getting to his knees, groping for his pistol, which had fallen from his hand. Then he realized his danger, for other horsemen and wagons were thundering down upon him. He began running.

His brother Lige came spurring to his rescue on the bay horse. Chick Nello caught an arm and swung up behind his brother. Then both were lost to view in the dust and phalanx of riders and vehicles as the avalanche swept onward, deeper into the new country.

"He killed his own horse," Della shouted above the uproar. "And he tried to kill you again!" She repeated that word, "Again!" She suddenly began to weep. "They'll try it again," she wept. "They'll never give up. You'll have to—to kill them—or be killed. They're that kind. Sonny told me."

"Is Sonny down there?" Vance shouted back.

She waved the question aside. Vance did not pursue it. He did not want an answer.

138

"At least we've shaken them off," he finally said.

"No," she replied. She pointed. A rider on a black mount was visible not far to their right, lost at times among the horde of riders and vehicles, but always reappearing. He was Art Nello on the black mare. He was paralleling their course, keeping them in sight. His brothers were lost somewhere amid the uproar back of them.

Della now began pushing the roan. The blazeface, which had been fighting restraint, relished the chance to stretch out and tried to pull away from the roan. When Vance again held it down, forcing it to let the roan set the pace, it began to sulk. Vance touched it with a spur. "None of that, my boy," he said. "This time you're playing second fiddle to another horse. A good horse."

They began to draw ahead of the mass of riders. So did Art Nello. Here and there on the prairie a few other men on fast horses were also emerging into the clear. The pace had slowed after the first frenzied rush, and was settling down to a matter of endurance.

Some of the stampeders were already dropping out to take possession of claims not far south of the deadline. Vance decided that they might be wiser than most, for it seemed to him that the prairie here appeared lush and fertile. But for the majority it was a case of distant fields being greener, or perhaps it was that the fever of the race had not worn off, for they were continuing their stampede, hell-bent, toward the southern horizon.

Driverless teams were running wild. Vance saw the front trucks of wagons bouncing along back of runaways, relics of vehicles whose reaches had broken in the race across prairie made treacherous by buffalo wallows and dry rain gullies.

Della was now slanting their course slightly westward

across the oncoming face of the rush. Art Nello was following suit. Vance judged that they had covered a mile, and the horses were beginning to slow to a jog. The world back of them was a saffron cloud of dust, with the sun shining dimly through the curtain. Ahead lay untrammeled prairie that would not be vacant long.

The dust curtain was caught by the rise of the afternoon wind as the day's warmth took effect, and came sweeping to overtake the leaders in the race. The stampeders began to scatter now, and their ranks were thinning as more and more dropped out to possess claims, and more and more veered east or west.

General eastward direction began to set in. Vance had listened to talk in the Buffalo Palace when he had played poker, and understood that streams of considerable size lay in that direction. It had been the consensus that the best farmland would lie along those streams, and that was where the towns would be established. Therefore, true to the human instinct to go along with the crowd, the majority were veering eastward, where they would vie with each other for claims, and leave what Vance judged might be better land on the higher prairie to the wiser.

Della suddenly swung the roan around, heading back over the way they had come, into the face of the oncoming ranks of stampeders. Vance understood. They were hidden by the dust from Art Nello's sight. She was circling back in order to shake him off.

They veered in a full circle, dodging among lumbering wagons, narrowly escaping collisions with other riders and buggies, many of whom had lost all sense of direction and were merely following each other in the herd instinct that was beginning to decide the destiny of the majority.

"What do you think?" Della asked.

Vance peered around through the yellow fog. "I think you've lost him," he said.

They veered directly south once more, but remained under cover among lumbering wagons for a time. This respite gave the horses a chance to recuperate.

Vance left the decisions up to Della, continuing to hold the impatient blazeface down and to let the roan lead the way. The country was vast, and it was now beginning to swallow the human flood. The dust thinned, and soon they were comparatively alone. Riders and wagons were in sight in every direction, but they were growing small against the might of the land. Vance and the girl began coming upon claims that were already staked. Disputes were also already starting. At one point two men were mauling at each other with fists, while womenfolk danced around them, screaming and urging them on. The issue was as to which had reached a certain piece of ground first. There were other claims around that had not been taken, and were apparently equally desirable, but the one over which they fought was the only one worth having, and was to be defended—perhaps to death.

Gunfire crackled, and the winks of powder flame came from another claim where a wagon had been overturned, and a man lay back of it with his huddled family, defending his right to this piece of land against what seemed to be three attackers. Looking back, Vance could see cavalrymen coming up at a gallop to the trouble spot. He and Della rode on.

"We better give the horses another breather," he said after another mile, veering their course toward a stand of brush alongside a small creek which held a seep of water.

Della started to protest, then gave in to the necessity,

and they halted in the shade, dismounted, and let the animals drink moderately. Della paced around, scanning the surroundings. There was no sign of the Nellos, no sign of danger.

"How far?" Vance asked.

"A few miles," she said.

Vance waited. It was time for some sort of showdown, some explanation from her.

"Do you want to tell me who this man is?" he finally said, desperately, when she remained silent.

She gazed at him, her eyes suddenly glistening with tears. "It would not be a favor to you," she said.

Again the stone wall. Vance had not known until this moment how deeply he was in love with this enigmatic person. Not until he was face to face with the realization that she soon would be lost to him. A few miles, so she had said.

He suddenly uttered a murmur for silence. Three horsemen were passing by on the prairie at a distance west of them. The Nello brothers. Chick Nello had managed to find a new mount for himself and had joined his brothers. Vance's surmise was that he had taken it by force from some boomer.

The Nellos were peering ahead as though hoping to sight their quarry to the south. They rode on, their horses moving at the sluggish half trot of animals that had seen hard miles.

Vance was not sure but what the Nellos had known he and Della were watching them from cover. "I doubt it," he said, voicing his thoughts aloud. "But they're smart. They guessed we'd circled, and they figured they'd pick us up eventually if they kept going south."

"They're devils," Della said exhaustedly. "And the devil is driving them. They'll kill you. It's hopeless. The odds are too great."

"You and your father knew they were in Gone Tomorrow all the time, didn't you?" Vance asked.

"Yes. We haven't had a moment they weren't watching us since—since . . ."

She faltered at saying it. Vance said it for her: "Since your brother got away with the money that night they held up the train."

"Yes," she said wearily.

"How about the map? It was a map, wasn't it? Doesn't that tell them where the money is?"

"It covers only a small area. First they have to know which creek to follow, and then to look for a landmark, which is a tangle of timber felled by a cyclone. If they knew that, they'd stop hounding me and my father. The map begins at that landmark."

"Well, I'm happy to know that you can trust me enough to tell me that much, at least," Vance said.

"Trust you?" she cried. "Why—I—I—" He felt that she was about to make some great emotional revelation. But she held it back. "Go back," she said, and her voice was heavy with emotion. "Don't get any deeper into this. Please. If the Nellos don't kill you, the Wells Fargo men will send you to prison. Yes, we have known for a long time that the express detectives have been watching us too, and for the same reason as the Nellos."

"You know, of course," Vance said huskily, "why I'm here? You must know."

She looked at him, her eyes swimming with tears. Suddenly, she drew close, put her arms around him and kissed him tenderly. "I know," she said. "And it will be on my conscience all my life if, because of me, anything happens to you."

"Does this man mean that much to you?" he asked.

"I can't tell you," she sobbed. She leaned against the roan, trying to hide her emotions.

Vance gave it up. His questions only tortured her. He still could not understand. After a time he said, "All right. We better move on."

"You must go back," she said. She had gained control of herself, and seemed determined to show him only an impersonal aspect. "I insist on it."

"No," Vance said.

He offered a hand into the saddle, and after a moment she decided to accept it, and mounted. He swung aboard the blazeface. Both horses had benefited by the rest, and Vance was sure they were in shape to hold their own against any animals the Nellos rode. By this time weaker stock was giving out, and weaker men also. Only the strong were still heading south.

Topping a rise, Vance peered, but could see no sign of the Nellos. But the country ahead was more broken and crossed by streams, with patches of timber here and there. It was possible, even probable, that the Nellos had taken cover in one of those hiding places ahead, both to rest their horses and in hope of sighting their quarry.

He was also wondering about the Wells Fargo agents and Marshal Ben Wheat. Apparently, they too had been thrown off the scent when he and Della had circled back. Looking north, he could see scattered boomers on the prairie. Lighter wagons and buggies were appearing now, but the general trend was still east of them.

He again let Della lead the way as they moved off the rise into the open. "Off to the left there seems to be gullies and some timber," he said.

She took the hint and headed in that direction. They found a small creek, along whose course the horses splashed and spattered mud and water, and whose cutbanks and brush offered cover. They followed this for a mile or more, then left it when it swung directly east instead of south.

The sun was casting long shadows. They had now been six hours on their way. It became necessary to rest the horses more often. Their progress had slowed to a plodding walk.

The sun went down. The prairie was bathed in translucent twilight, laden with the sweetness of blooming spring. A band of deer burst from a swale ahead, and hopscotched over hummocks of brush, vanishing into new cover. A cloud of mallards, teel and pintails arose from a marshy pond that lay athwart their path. They let the horses drink here. The limbs of pecan trees drooped with the weight of turkeys, seeking roosting places for the night.

"How much farther?" Vance finally asked.

"I didn't tell you the truth when you asked that before," she said. "I had hoped you would turn back. It's still quite a distance."

"Two miles? Three? Five?"

"Farther than that."

"You don't want to tell me, do you?"

"I still hope you'll listen to me and go back." She looked at him gravely. "There must be other girls waiting for you. Are there?"

"I'd be a fool to answer that."

"Are there?"

"Dozens," Vance snorted. "I've got a pretty girl yearning for me in every town on the border."

"No doubt. We're speaking of something else. Of love. You are supposed to be a gunman, a crooked gambler, a killer. How many men have you really killed?"

"That's got nothing to do with this."

"I doubt if you ever killed anyone. You're a fraud, Vance Barret. Oh, I imagine you are very efficient with a gun. Very fast. You have had to be to stay alive in the manner in which you live—by your wits. But that isn't the reputation you really want, deep inside you. You started searching for something else in life, but because you're the son of an outlaw, peace officers have dogged you, watched you, warned you, and you felt that you had to live up to what they expected of you. You dressed like a gambler, called the bluff of toughs who tried to back you down, and spent your time in dancehalls and saloons. And you never really felt at home there."

"My God!" Vance exclaimed. "Are you some kind of an evangelist? Are you trying to convert me to a better way of life?"

"No, I'm Princess Delilah, the fortuneteller, and I can see your future unless you come out of this romantic dream that you are in love with me and are therefore obligated to see this through."

"So you think that's all it is—a romantic dream?" Vance asked. "What if I happened to be making a fool of you? What if it's the money I want, after all?"

"I've told you before that it's yours."

"You always bring me up against a blank wall," Vance said. "And I tell you again I don't want it."

"Have you ever seen eighty thousand dollars—all in one pile. All in crisp, sound bank notes?"

"And you? Have you?"

"Have I what?" But she knew what he meant. After a moment she said quietly, "Yes, I've seen it. All of it in one pile. I warn you it does things to you. There's greed

146

in everyone. There's the hope of being rich. The devil put those things in every human mind. I know what I'm talking about. I've been tempted."

"You actually *saw* that money?"

She did not answer for a time. "Yes," she finally said. "I've been there."

"Been there? Where? You mean you've been to the cache? You've been in the Territory before this? When?"

"Weeks ago. I've lost track of time."

"You don't want to tell me about it, do you?"

"No," she said. "What good would it do? All I want is for you to turn back. You will be tempted also."

"If you've been to this place, you know exactly where we are going and how to get there, don't you? You don't need a map."

"No. I made the map. It was only in case my father needed it."

"Then you know exactly how far away it is?"

"I'd say at least twenty-five miles," she said.

"Twenty-five miles? You know it's going to be dark in half an hour."

"We can throw off and wait until daylight."

"It would be better to keep going, if possible. But risky. The country ahead looks rough. But it would be a good bet for avoiding the Nellos."

"And the Fargos," she said.

"And the Fargos. You can count on them picking up your trail sooner or later. It's a sure bet they'll have Indian trackers to call in."

They remained under cover until deep dusk settled, then pushed ahead again. Crickets began their rhythmic beat. Frogs croaked behind them in the pond, the sound fading into other night calls. Bats darted overhead. The first fireflies of the season lighted their tiny candles around them.

There were also human sounds. In the distance they sighted the ruddy glow of campfires on the open prairie where boomers had staked claims, or had thrown off for the night. They avoided these.

The night was black. There was no moon, only a blaze of stars overhead, a blaze so brilliant that it only seemed to deepen the crushing darkness around them. Vance could scarcely make out the outline of the brush just a few strides ahead of his mount. He slowed the pace to a cautious walk. Even so, the blazeface pitched forward into an unseen, small gully. The depression was only two or three feet deep, and the animal recovered without leg injury. Vance was nearly unseated, but managed to hang on and right himself in the saddle.

"This is ridiculous," he said.

"It's worse than that," Della said. "I'm lost."

Vance peered into the sky, located the pointers on the Big Dipper, and lined up the North Star. "At least we're still heading south," he said.

A cold wind sprang up. The greening grass and the brush around them came to life with ghostly moaning and rustling. Clouds moved in, obscuring the stars, erasing their last guidepost.

Vance called a halt. "We're in for weather," he said. "We camp here. We'll only get lost wandering around in this sort of featherbed."

He stumbled around on foot until he located a stand of thick oak, and led the animals into shelter. The rain came before he could finish unsaddling. He and Della huddled together against the bole of an oak, but the rain, driven by the wind, came in a torrent, and they were soon soaked to the skin. They fought it out in mutual misery. Vance was feeling the strain of the day. The physical part of it was insignificant compared to the mental stress.

The Nellos had been shaken off for the time being, but there were three of them, and they would have that advantage in sweeping the country to pick up trace of their quarry. Now that the storm had intervened, daybreak was sure to overtake them long before they could cover the distance she had mentioned, increasing the chances of being sighted by their pursuers manyfold.

In spite of his discomfort, he must have dozed off, for the downpour had ended when he aroused. He spoke. "The clouds are breaking. We can saddle up soon and make a few miles before the sun catches us."

There was no answer. He reached out. His hand touched only the bole of the tree. Della had been there beside him when he had dozed. Now she was gone!

He leaped to his feet, finding his legs stiffened by the chill of the storm. "Della!" he called.

There was no answer. He stumbled to where he had tethered the horses. The blazeface was missing, along with the saddle she had been using on the roan. She could not have left many minutes ago, but he knew there would be little chance of finding her in the darkness—and less chance of overtaking her on the slower roan. And to force her into a race in the darkness likely would have only one result. A fall—a broken neck perhaps.

CHAPTER 12

VANCE FORCED HIMSELF TO WAIT. THE STORM WAS moving east. Stars were showing through breaking clouds. He finally located the North Star. Saddling, adjusting the stirrups, he mounted and rode south, letting the roan pick its way at a slow pace.

She had warned him repeatedly to turn back, had indicated that something like this would happen. "Have you ever seen eighty thousand dollars all in one pile?" she had asked. She did not believe he could resist the temptation, just as she was not resisting it, evidently. She had seen the money, been exposed to its power. Now she was on her way to what apparently was an arranged meeting place with "Sonny" at a point where the booty was cached.

More than once, Vance pulled the roan to a stop while he sat, torn by conflicting impulses. Common sense kept telling him to turn back, as she had warned him to do. There were times when he started to swing the roan around and head over his backtrail—back to find Iggy and Jim Leatherwood, back to the familiar life of a gypsy gambler who lived by hook or crook. It was a life that had more valleys than peaks, but in it a man had no such harsh decisions to make as this one—this one that he had been told might cost him his life—and for what? For a girl who mistrusted him, and whose loyalty and love was not for him.

But each time he would pull up again and sit for a time, unable to continue with this retreat. He always veered the roan south again. He could not help himself. Even though this was the second time she had stolen a horse and tried to part from him and his help, he could not bring himself to let her ride alone.

Daybreak dimmed the stars, turned remnant clouds of the storm into galleons of gold in a turquoise sky. The tiny silhouette of a lone rider appeared on a swell to the west, vanished, reappeared again. Hope sprang in him, then died. That distant figure wore a narrow-brimmed, flat-crowned hat. A man.

There were newly occupied claims, marked by fresh

stakes which bore streamers, and the names of the claimants were penciled, carved or painted on the shafts. The flat ahead was likely-looking farmland, but beyond the stream, which cut across the land, rose stony hills, scabbed with scrub oak, locust and straggly pecan. No boomer would bother with that barren-looking land when there was richer soil to be had nearer at hand. The country beyond the creek was where the lone rider had appeared.

The rider appeared again. He was not alone. Two more horsemen came in sight, then vanished into the breaks of the hills. There was no doubt in Vance's mind as to their identity. The Nellos. The fact that they were riding together indicated that they might have picked up the trail of their quarry, and now were following by sight.

"Did you see a young fellow ride by here on a blazeface chestnut?" Vance asked a sleep-eyed boomer who was building his breakfast fire on his claim.

He had to repeat the question three times as he rode across the flats, past other staked claims. A man with a Down East twang finally allowed that such a person had passed by on a tired blazeface.

"How long ago?"

"Half, three quarters of an hour, mister," the man said.

Vance pushed the roan. It could not respond with any spirit. But now he picked up tracks. He had shaped the shoes on the chestnut animal. The calks were sharp, the trail easy to follow in the rain-wet earth.

The trail crossed the creek and mounted into the scraggy hills, following a pocket between the ridges, heading west for a mile or so. Then, as the pocket continued on westward, Della had swung the blazeface up a slant to a divide, and descended from the hogback

151

to easier going to the south.

Vance tried to argue with himself that the three riders he had sighted had not been the Nellos, but only boomers seeking greener pastures to the south. He failed to convince himself.

A flight of turkey rose from cover near the rocky rim of a ridge, so far distant that the heavy drumfire of wings was only a distant rumble in his ears. Something—or someone—had flushed the fowls. A few minutes later a cloud of wild pigeons arose from another point.

If it was the Nellos who had spooked the flocks, there could no longer be any doubt but that they had spotted Della and were tracing her route southward. Furthermore, Vance knew that he also would surely be sighted by the brothers if he continued following the tracks of the blazeface into the open. That would mean certain ambush.

From cover he surveyed the terrain, and decided he might escape detection if he swung farther west. That meant considerable loss of distance and time. The roan was game, and good for miles yet, but the blazeface evidently was even stronger, for the marks of the shoes were deeper at the crown, showing that Rajah was still stepping out with some energy. Della's lighter weight was a big factor in measuring the capability of the horses.

Vance mentally balanced the odds with the same cold judgment he would use in deciding whether to bet or drop out of a poker pot. He might move directly ahead, bait the Nellos into a gun battle in which the odds would be heavily against him, or he could risk the chance of losing sight of Della entirely by veering off the trail.

His decision was that Della was safe enough—for the

time being. She was the only person who could lead the Nellos to the train-robbery loot. Alive, she was worth eighty thousand dollars to them—until they had the money in their hands. As for himself, the Nellos would kill him on sight. Indeed, they would likely go out of their way to get rid of him. Thanks to his reputation as a gunman, they would, no doubt, likely prefer to do this by ambush or treachery.

He gambled with the odds. Better to put off the showdown than to risk losing everything by riding straight ahead and playing their game. He swung the roan away. The going was slow through thick undergrowth on heavy slants, and he was finally forced to dismount and fight it through on foot to spare the horse.

Reaching better going below the slope, he mounted again. He followed a draw whose shoulders rose between him and where he had seen the Nellos. He swung south, hoping he had made the right gamble. The sun drew clear of the horizon. Its warmth brought mists rising from the rain-soaked prairie. Soon he rode in a blanket of pale fog. Thin at first, it thickened so that he rode through a damp, gray featherbed. For a time he had no sense of direction.

Then a pale-yellow eye looked down at him through the gray cloak. The sun! He stood up in the stirrups, and his head emerged from a pallid sea that stretched eerily around him. It was a ground fog that in many places was no deeper than the height of a man standing in stirrups on horseback. He saw the ridges and hogbacks close at hand. It was in that direction that the trail of Della's mount had been heading.

The fog protected him from observation. He crouched back into its folds, letting the roan pick its way.

153

Occasionally, where the mist clung close to the ground, he let his head emerge so as to make sure of his bearings.

Reaching higher ground, he rode clear of the cloying blanket. Looking back, the prairie was a ghost ground, hiding boomers, animals, hollows and brush.

Keeping to what cover he could find, he circled eastward. Presently he came upon the sign of horses. Several of them. He followed the faint traces until the hoofmarks became plain in a stretch of wet ground. The shoes of three of the animals were worn by use. The tracks of the fourth horse had been made by the blazeface.

His first freezing thought was that the Nellos had taken Della prisoner, and were forcing her to lead them to their objective. After he had followed the trail for a distance, he saw that this was not the case. The three horses with the worn shoes had veered away from the route taken by the blazeface, and had headed for a rise slightly to the north. Della's mount had continued ahead, following a swale.

The Nellos had been following the tracks left by her mount, and evidently had drawn so close that they had elected to move to higher ground and try to keep her in sight from cover. Vance decided that she must not be aware that the Nellos had picked up her trail and were so close at hand.

He found another draw, shallow but adequate to offer cover, which roughly paralleled the direction Della had taken some half a mile away. It carried him into an area of broken hills, veined with dry drainage channels and matted with heavy tangles of brush and timber. Reaching a crest, he saw open country ahead, threaded by a sizable stream along which brush and tall trees flourished.

He glimpsed Della and the blazeface. They were a mere dot at that distance, crawling buglike across a greening flat toward the timber of the stream. This stream, Vance guessed, must be the one that would lead to the storm-downed stretch of trees that was the key to the treasure map.

There could be no doubt but that the Nellos, peering from some vantage point, would be following her progress also. The girl and the horse vanished into the brush along the stream. Vance waited for a time, because open ground lay beyond the stream, waiting to see if she reappeared in that direction. Far to the north arose the thin streamer of campfire smoke, indicating that some boomer had made it that far. No doubt others would be moving in as the day advanced, but the terrain to the south seemed to lie vacant as far as Vance could determine—awaiting the second-day wave of settlers, who would stake the remaining claims surely before nightfall. Della was racing time, racing the onrush of boomers, racing the Nellos.

She did not reappear. That meant she was following the course of the stream. Vance continued to wait. Presently, he sighted three horsemen emerging from the hills far to his left. They were the Nellos. They vanished, reappeared, vanished. They were heading for the timber into which the girl had gone.

To keep within reasonable distance of them, Vance was forced to chance crossing an open flat. On one occasion he found himself in plain sight of the three riders. They were a long distance away, and he could not tell whether they were looking in his direction. He took cover as soon as possible and waited, watching.

The brothers kept moving steadily toward the timber

155

and entered its shadows. Vance debated it. They might not have seen him. On the other hand . . . it could be an ambush, and they might be waiting to pick him off.

He worked his way nearer the timber, which lay silent—menacing in his path. He dismounted. The roan had about reached its limit. He believed he could travel faster on foot than on the tired animal. He drew his rifle from the sling, then searched around and found dry lengths of limbs which he formed into a crude cross, lashing the pieces together with strings cut from his saddle blanket with his pocketknife. He draped his coat over this arrangement, stuffing it with dead leaves and grass to give it a semblance of reality, then topped it off with his hat.

The roan snorted in protest when he began lashing this makeshift scarecrow upright in the saddle, but its nature was docile, and it was too utterly weary to offer real protest. Vance sacrificed the sleeves of his shirt to make additional strings with which to hold the effigy in place.

"If they kill you, old friend," Vance said, "I'll never forgive myself."

He turned the roan loose. The animal stood, puzzled, refusing to be deserted, but Vance swung it around, headed it out of the covert, giving it a slap on the rump. The roan, astonished and its pride hurt, trotted out of the brush into the open. Vance waited without much hope that his makeshift arrangement would stay in place long enough to serve the purpose for which it had been created.

The roan slowed to a walk, then stopped and started to crop at the new grass. Then the scarecrow toppled. In Vance's ears was the crack of a rifle. The bullet had come from the timber two hundred yards away. The marksman's bead had been perfect, for the effigy pitched headlong from the saddle, then dangled there. The startled roan, galvanized into a last burst of strength, pitched and sunfished and kicked until it broke free of the terrible dangling thing.

Vance remained under cover. The Nellos might have realized they had been tricked. They might not. Nothing more happened. No sound came from the timber, no head appeared. Vance waited minute after minute. A quarter of an hour. He finally was forced, by the passing of time, to make a move. He crawled through the high grass, carrying the rifle, ready to shoot, knowing that it was impossible to conceal his position. No opposition came. The thickets into which the Nellos had gone along the stream remained silent. He decided that they either believed they had killed him, or felt that they had no time to risk making sure. Della Judson was building up distance on them with each lost minute.

Vance found a small ravine, which offered cover, and moved along it. He had traveled only a few hundred yards when he rounded a bend in the gully and came face to face with—Della Judson.

She was on foot. Her eyes were great pools of despair. He had lifted the rifle, his finger on the trigger. It was an instinctive move, for it was only the Nellos he had expected to encounter.

Her expression changed from that of lost hope to wild joy. He lowered the rifle. Before he could speak she rushed to him, threw her arms around him and buried her face against his cheek, which was rough with the two-day stubble of dark beard.

"I—I thought you were dead," she sobbed. "I saw them shoot you. I saw you fall."

"It was only a scarecrow I rigged on the roan to draw their fire," he said. "Stop it. Get hold of yourself. You shouldn't have turned back. What about Son—about the

157

money?"

She continued to cling to him, sobbing, unable to speak for a time. "You're alive," she chattered finally. "You're alive! You're alive!"

He shook her until she calmed. "Where's the runner?" he asked. "Rajah?"

She again was unable to speak coherently. She took him by the hand, as though he were a small child who needed her protection, and led him down the ravine a short distance to where the chestnut horse stood, reins on the ground.

"I had started to circle back," she said, forcing herself to speak intelligibly. "I was trying to lead them away from the—the place. Then I saw them shoot you."

"You knew they were trailing you?"

"Not until the last few miles. I felt sure up to that time that I had lost them. I was wrong. I caught a glimpse of them entering the timber along the stream. All I could do was to try to lead them away. They have the map, you know."

"You mean it's near—the place?"

"Very near. Too near."

Again she took his hand. Vance caught up the reins of the blazeface and let her lead both of them. They emerged abruptly into an area that was a phalanx of fallen timber. A cyclone had ripped a narrow path of destruction across the creek in the past. Della skirted this hazard and they entered a small tributary stream, thickly brushed. They waded in the icy water, pushing through overhanging willows.

"We're there," she said.

The brush faded, and Vance looked out over a grassy meadow, enclosed by low, brushy ridges. A few locust, pecan and oak dotted the flat, which was rich with the greening of spring. An enormous bur oak spread branches over a bubbling spring which was the source of the small stream.

The basin appeared to be empty. Yet it had that aura that indicated the presence of humans. A faint footpath led to the spring, the tang of woodsmoke was in the air. Then Vance saw it—the opening into a dugout that was backed into the face of a small ridge not far from the spring.

Della led the way closer to that habitation and called out, "Sonny! Bobbie!"

A shadow moved in the opening. Vance saw the glint of a rifle barrel. "Who's that with you, Della?" a man's voice demanded.

"A friend," she said. "Put down the gun. We've come with a horse. A good horse."

She rushed ahead. The man came into the open to meet her. He was hobbling on a twisted, bootless leg, using a cane for support. He was young, and as lean and bony as a coyote. His hair was long. A scraggly beard masked his jaws.

Vance watched Della rush into the arms of this wild man. She was sobbing again and uttering mothering sounds. "Sonny! Sonny!" she wept. "You look terrible. Your leg—"

"I'll never walk on it again," the man said. "But I'm alive, though I wonder why."

"Thank God, I got here in time," Della sobbed.

159

CHAPTER 13

A SECOND PERSON CAME FROM THE DOOR OF THE dugout. She wore the calico blouse, full woolen skirt, headband and moccasins of an Osage girl, but she was not an Indian, although her skin was deeply tanned. She was about eighteen.

She rushed into Della's arms. "Bobbie!" Della wept. "Oh, Bobbie! There were times when I never expected to see either of you alive again. So many, many times."

"Where's Father?" the younger girl asked.

"He's safe. I'll tell you about it later."

The young bearded man leaned on his cane and on the rifle, looking at Vance. "And just who are you?" he asked.

"I'm not sure," Vance said. "You are Sonny, I take it?"

"That's what my sisters and my father call me," he said.

"Your *sisters?*"

"I'm Frank Judson. Della and Bobbie are my sisters. Bobbie's real name is Roberta."

Vance ran a sleeve over his brow to clear away the cobwebs. He was recalling now that Leatherwood had mentioned something about Henry Judson having had three children back in those days in Santa Fe long ago.

"You're supposed to be dead, Judson," he finally said. "I got that from information that is usually reliable."

"There've been times I wished I was," Frank Judson said. "I guess I'm lucky to be alive, lucky to have a leg at all. But I earned it. I got no complaints. I—"

160

"There's no time for talk now," Della exclaimed, turning from her sister's embrace. "Can you ride, Sonny? Is your leg well enough?"

"Yes," Frank Judson said. "I sure can't walk very far. All I need is a horse."

Della was looking at Vance. He turned and eyed the blazeface. The past two days had taken weight off it, bringing out the haunch sinews. But its head was still up. It still had a touch of fire in its eyes.

"Where's the money?" Della asked.

Frank Judson's lips twisted into a bitter smile "So that's the price?" he said. "It's in there—in the dugout. It's all yours, mister, whatever your name is. I want no part of it. Never did. I sort of came into looking after it by accident. I had intended to give it back at first chance."

"Back?" Vance asked.

"To Wells Fargo," Frank Judson said. "I warn you that it's money that will never do you any good. Blood money never does."

"Get it, Bobbie," Della said. "Hurry. The Nellos are around. They'll show up sooner or later. Sonny, can you make it alone? Should I go with you? Or Bobbie? I've got a little money for you. Our own money. Judson money."

"I can make it," Frank Judson said. He eyed the blazeface. "But I doubt if that horse has got many more miles in him—at least until he's rested."

"He's still the best horse around," Vance said. "He has outrun them all, and he'll outrun them again."

The younger girl came from the dugout, dragging two bulging leather *mochilas* by their straps.

"My brother was a fool," Della said. "And he probably still is. But he's still my brother. I just couldn't let him be killed by the Nellos, or caught by the express detectives. And I feared for Bobbie above all. I couldn't

161

tell you these things before. In the first place, you'd never have believed me."

"And in the second place, you didn't trust me," Vance said.

"Sonny was drunk the night he rode with the Nellos. He didn't know their real identity. They were using other names at the time. He was young and wild and liked to hang around with that sort of men, hoping the toughness would rub off on him. He thought he was going to a *baile* at a ranch outside of town. The first thing he knew, he was holding their horses while they were blowing the express safe in a Santa Fe train at a water tank. And then he was riding away with all the horses and with another fool named Clem Barker."

"Do you have to be so hard on me, Sis," Frank Judson demanded weakly. "I wasn't as—"

Della ignored him. "The Nellos were shooting at them. Clem Barker died of his wounds the next day. Sonny had a bullet in his leg. It shattered the bone below the knee. He managed to send word to us, and Bobbie and I found him and took care of him until he could be moved. We knew he was being hunted high and low by the Nellos. He still had the money with him. He wanted to give himself up, but we knew what that would have meant. Those two men who were murdered were well-known and well-liked. And we couldn't think of any way of returning the money without bringing the law down on Sonny, and maybe a lynch mob. I guess we weren't thinking very straight. We didn't want Father to know. We were afraid of what he might do. Whether you believe it or not, he is a very upright man, even though he does sell sugar pap as medicine. That is only to keep from starvation, and actually, the people who buy it get their money's worth in the show he puts on. At any rate,

162

Bobbie and I disguised ourselves as Indian girls, got food and a camp pack and carried Sonny clear across the Cherokee Strip on a travois drawn by an Indian pony. We kept him covered with old buffalo hides and got him to this place. We knew about this dugout, for we had camped here some years ago with Father when we were moving from Texas to Dodge City."

"The cavalry?" Vance asked.

"This was weeks ago. There weren't as many cavalrymen in the Territory, and what there were kept too busy stopping white sooners to worry about Indians. They didn't even stop us to question us. Sonny was more dead than alive when we got here. After he began to pull through, I left Bobbie with him and went back to Kansas, riding the Indian pony, to find Father. You know the rest."

"A very pretty story," Vance said. "You almost have me believing it. If your father had camped here once, why was the map necessary?"

Her lips were tight. "I don't blame you for not believing me," she said. "I wasn't sure he could remember the place. And the trees had been downed by the storm since that time. I also was not sure I might live to get back. For I found out that the Nellos were watching Father. Then they started to watch both of us."

Frank Judson's rifle swung up, leveled on Vance's heart. "I'm taking that horse, mister," he said. "I don't give a hoot what you believe. You came for the money. You've got it."

Della pushed the gun down, then wrested it from her brother's hands, "It won't be that way!" she said. "It is his horse—his decision."

She looked at Vance. "This kind of money won't buy the horse, will it?" she said. "What will?"

Vance gazed at her for a space. "He doesn't deserve it," he said. "He doesn't deserve sisters like you two." He turned to Frank Judson. "There's no price, no price at all. Only be as easy on that gelding as you can be. You'll never mount a better horse. Take him. And don't waste time. You can be in Texas in a few days. After that, you've got all the room in the world to hide in."

Frank Judson looked at his sisters and said, "I can't—" He quit talking, because he didn't really mean it.

"You needn't pretend to worry about them," Vance said. "They haven't robbed any trains. They're not wanted by the law."

"The money?" Judson said. "I could use a few of those bank notes."

"I'll show you what to do with that sort of money," Vance said. "You pretended you wanted to give it back to its rightful owners, didn't you? I'll show you how."

He walked to the *mochilas*, seized the straps, and dragged the bags out into the basin some fifty yards from the dugout. He freed the buckles. Frank Judson started to voice an outraged cry of protest, but his sister silenced him.

Vance upended the contents of the *mochilas* into the grass. The train-robbery loot came out in a flood. It was all in yellow-backed gold notes. The bills had been packeted originally, but many of the packets had been broken during their travels. Bills fluttered in the soft wind. Solid packets of yellow-backs lay in a heap in the spring sun.

Vance tossed the *mochilas* aside and left the heap of money lying there. He walked back to the dugout. The girls had stood silent. Frank Judson still acted as though stunned.

Suddenly the girls understood. "The Nellos!" Della exclaimed. "Hurry, Frank! Hurry, Bobbie!"

Bobbie raced into the dugout. Vance, peering in, saw

164

that she was frantically getting together a pack of food, along with blankets and cooking utensils. Della produced a wallet and handed it over to her brother. "There's two hundred dollars in it," she said. "Once you make it across Red River you'll be in Texas. Mexico would be safer until we are sure how things go."

Frank Judson weakly tried to protest, to say that he couldn't hide back of petticoats, and that he'd stay and take his medicine like a man. Then he burst into tears. He kissed his sisters, babbling that he didn't deserve their loyalty. He started to offer his hand to Vance, then withdrew it, realizing that it would be refused. He tossed the gunny sack of equipment across the horse, pulled himself into the saddle, and rode away without another word.

Vance stood there between two young women who wept and wept and wept for a brother they did not expect to see again.

Della finally dried her eyes. "He'll grow up someday," she said. She looked at Vance. "And now you know everything."

"Now I know," he said.

Bobbie spoke. "At least I ought to be introduced. I don't even know your name, tall man."

"Call me Vance, and I'll be happy to answer," Vance said.

"I'm not a real Indian, you know," Bobbie said. "When I get these duds off and get gussied up, some folks might even think I am pretty."

"You're wasting your time, Bobbie," Della said, laughing. "He's spoken for."

"By whom?"

A rifle bullet snapped past and tore through the pole wall that fronted the dugout. From the snapping sound, Vance knew the slug had been meant for him and had

165

missed by inches.

He seized both girls and pushed them toward the door of the dugout. "Run!"

More slugs ripped furrows in the earth around them and damaged the face of the dugout, but they dove through the narrow opening uninjured. The girls landed in a heap, and Vance plummeted on top of them.

The Nellos had arrived. Vance wriggled free of the girls and shoved them away from the opening. More bullets were finding the interior of the dugout.

"Stay down!" Vance said. "Stay clear of the door!"

Slugs continued to hammer the dugout. Its floor had been excavated some eighteen inches below the surface, and they had that protection until the storm of lead subsided.

The dugout was small, gloomy. A rude rock fireplace had been built at the rear, with an opening dug through the face of the ridge to permit smoke to escape. The fire was still alive. A bullet struck in the embers, kicking up a shower of sparks.

Another slug pierced the smoke-blackened coffeepot on the hearth, spilling its contents into the ashes.

"The filthy rascals!" Bobbie Judson blazed. "Just look at our coffeepot. It's ruined!"

The shooting ended. Vance looked anxiously at his companions. All of them had escaped unscathed. In the dust-fogged dimness he made out more details of the interior. Two pallets had been arranged in a double-bunk framework of poles, lashed with rawhide. The remains of a haunch of venison hung in a corner. Dried jerky was skewered on twigs overhead. He discovered that Bobbie was producing two rifles from somewhere, along with ammunition, and arming herself and Della.

166

Bobbie read his dubious expression correctly. "Don't be afraid we'll shoot you by accident," she sniffed. "We've done some hunting in our day."

"Your day must have been pretty recent," Vance said. "How old are you? About seventeen?"

"Old enough to know how to pull a trigger," Bobbie said.

"What now?" Della asked, peering through one of the openings bullets had torn in the pole supports.

"Seems like it's up to them," Vance said.

A voice was raised in the brush. "That's you in there, ain't it, Frank? Come on out. We're here to collect. Fetch out the money. That's all we want. Then we'll go away." The speaker was Chick Nello.

"Answer him," Vance said to Della.

"Frank isn't here," she called.

"Don't try to give us that," Nello yelled. "We jest seen him with our own eyes."

"You're mistaken," Della replied. "Frank's been long gone from here. You'll never see him again."

Chick Nello's response was to send another rifle bullet through the pole wall. The slug buried itself in the earth at the rear. More dust drifted from the ceiling.

"Come out, or we'll shoot that rat nest full of holes!" Nello shouted. "We ain't been shootin' to kill up to now, but we ain't long on patience. All we want is that money, Frank. Hand it over, an' we'll let all of you go."

Vance lifted his voice. "Frank Judson isn't here, Chick. But I am."

There was a space of silence. Then he could hear the brothers talking profanely back and forth. Apparently, they were stationed at various points where their guns could command the dugout from all directions.

"You don't happen to be that Barret tinhorn what

dealt himself into this thing?" Chick Nello demanded.

"Or his ghost," Vance answered. "You put a bullet right through my hat a while back, Chick. And it isn't the first time you've acted like I was a duck in a shooting gallery. Now, is that being nice?"

"Hey, Chick!" one of the brothers screeched. "Look! Thar in the open between us an' thet dugout door! Thet yalla paper! Ain't thet—ain't thet—by Gawd, it *is* money!"

Again a moment of utter silence on the part of the Nellos. "What in *the* hell!" Chick Nello finally croaked.

Vance peered, trying to locate the positions of the brothers. But the brush, a rifle shot away, was too dense. He failed.

The breeze was scattering loose bank notes about in the grass. One of the Nellos uttered a moan. "It's gonna blow away! Do somethin', Chick!"

"Do somethin' yourself!" Chick raged.

Vance again tried to determine from where the voices were coming, without result. He did discover something else. The dugout stood on higher ground than the creek, and afforded a view of the flats to the north. Horsemen had appeared in the distance. They were too far away for him to make sure of their identity, but one of the riders, at least, was a bulky man. He could be Marshal Ben Wheat. If so, his companions, no doubt, were law officers also, and Wells Fargo agents.

"Come and get it, Chick," Vance shouted.

"Git what?"

"The money, of course. That's all you say you wanted. You earned it. Robbed a train and killed two men to get it. It's all yours, along with everything that goes with it."

"Bait, huh?" Chick Nello snarled. "Do you think I'm

168

soft enough to fall for that? The minute I show myself will be my last. I hear you're pretty quick with a gun, Barret."

"I never shot a man in cold blood in my life," Vance said. "I never will. Not even a ringhorn like you. I'll make a deal with you. None of us want any part of that money. All the Judsons want is to let you have it so that there won't be any reason for carrying on a grudge. They don't want to live the rest of their lives trying to hide from you. I'll count up to three. At the count of three, you and I will show ourselves. I'll stand by the dugout in plain sight while you come out and get the money. Your brothers could gun me down if I tried to run a sandy on you."

Again there was discussion among the brothers as to Vance's sincerity. "You an' Lige go out there, Art," Chick Nello finally said. "I'll lay a bead on Barret, in case he's up to somethin'."

"Why us?" Art Nello demanded. "What about you goin' out there?"

"I say for you to go," Chick Nello snarled. "I'm the best shot. Neither of you two kin hit the ground with your hats when you're under the gun."

"All the more reason why you're the one to go out," Lige yelled. "You got me an' Art into somethin' we didn't figure on when you gunned down them two men at the train. We didn't aim on bein' in on a hangin' job. If anybody goes out there, it's goin' to be you, Chick."

There was torrid debate, charges and countercharges among the brothers for a time. Chick grew frenziedly angry, threatening to lock up his brothers and use a gun on them, but they remained adamant. Chick was finally forced to give in.

"All right, Barret," he shouted. "It's a deal. I don't

169

give a hoot whether you live or die, or any of them Judsons either. All I want is what we earned—the *dinero.* You come out without any guns."

"No deal," Vance said. "If I come out, it's with my side gun handy. You can do the same if you wish."

"Not me," Chick said. "I'll come out clean. No gun. All I'm interested in is the money."

"Don't trust him," Della breathed.

Vance lifted his voice again. "I might mention a couple of things. There are two Judson girls here with rifles, and they know how to use them. If any of you have any notion about taking a snapshot at me, Chick will be the next one to get it. Secondly, some firebrands will be tossed onto that pile of money out there. Then there'll be no money for anyone. Do you hear me?"

"I hear you," Chick said. "Start your count."

Vance began the count. "One! Two! Three!"

He arose, stepped out of the doorway into the open. He crouched a little, ready to dive for cover. He half expected the Nellos to shoot. But he won the gamble. Chick Nello appeared from the brush across the flat. He had his arms lifted to show that they held no weapon, and Vance could see no holster on him.

"All right," Vance called.

Chick moved toward the money, slowly, suspiciously at first. Then he broke into a run. Reaching the heap of bank notes, he frenziedly began stuffing them into the *mochilas.* He finished storing the packets, then scrambled around, gathering up the wind-blown bills.

The task was almost completed when he whirled suddenly. He had a six-shooter in his hand. Evidently, he had concealed it in his shirt, waiting until he believed Vance was off guard. He meant to shoot to kill.

Vance's weapon was in the holster at his side. Chick

170

thought he had an easy kill and took an instant to make sure it would be a belly shot. That delay cost him his advantage.

Vance drew, firing as his gun leveled above the holster. His bullet struck its target an instant before Chick released the thumbed hammer of his Colt. The impact of the .44 slug tore a leg from beneath Chick, sending him whirling around to plunge on his face in the grass. His weapon exploded, the bullets tearing into the soil to Vance's left. That was the only shot Chick was able to fire. The shock of the injury blinded him then.

Vance plunged inside the dugout, expecting the two brothers to open up. But they did not. Chick Nello was trying to sit up. He was grabbing at his right leg and groaning in agony. Blood was beginning to flow. "Come here an' help me, you fools!" he shouted to his brothers.

"How bad are you hit?" Lige asked from cover.

"How'n hell do I know? I got it in the laig. I'm bleedin' mighty bad."

"Come and get him," Vance called. "Take him away from here. And the money too. I won't shoot you."

Art Nello finally ventured dubiously into the open. He scuttled across the open ground to where his older brother sat, clutching his leg. Lige followed. The two brothers stood looking down at Chick. And at the *mochilas,* bulging with loot.

Lige suddenly picked up Chick's pistol, which lay nearby in the grass. "Looks like you only got a flesh wound, Chick," he said. "Too bad. I was hopin' you was a goner. You know, I never did like any part o' you."

He lifted Chick's pistol, and Vance felt a chill of horror, for he thought Lige was about to shoot his brother. Then Lige decided not to go through with it. He thrust the gun in his belt. He and Art picked up the *mochilas* Without another word, they began running back toward the brush.

Chick sat there, staring. "Why, you yella cowards!" he finally croaked. "I'm your brother. Your brother, you hear! You mean you're leavin' me here, crippled, an' goin' away with all the money? My money?"

His brothers kept running away toward the brush. Chick tried to get to his feet, frothing with fury. He made it, then took a stride and fell again. He could only lie there, cursing his brothers as they vanished from sight. Vance heard the sound of hooves as they mounted and headed away.

The riders on the flat beyond the creek had drawn close now, so that there was no doubt about their identity. Ben Wheat with a posse.

Vance saw them pull their horses abruptly to a halt and snatch rifles from saddleboots. The two Nello brothers had emerged from the creek bottom—to find themselves trapped.

Lige Nello made a panicky mistake. He went for his side gun, drew and fired. One of the possemen staggered in the saddle. The possemen opened up. Lige fired a second time, but he was then riddled with bullets. He toppled lifeless from the saddle. Art Nello, who was riding the black mare, had known that it was hopeless from the first, and had lifted his arms in surrender. Vance watched the posse ride in and surround Art.

After a time, Ben Wheat and the posse rode up to the dugout. Two Pawnee trailers were in the group. Art Nello was with them, handcuffed, and the body of his brother was draped over a saddle.

The two girls were busy bandaging Chick Nello's wound. Vance's bullet had torn an ugly furrow through

172

Chick's leg just above the knee. One of the possemen, who wore a Wells Fargo badge, had a stained bandage on a forearm that was in an improvised sling. Another of the posse was leading Vance's roan, Pawnee.

Ben Wheat gazed from beneath grizzled brows at Vance, at the girls, at the dugout, at Chick Nello. He removed his hat. "Good mawnin', ladies," he said. "An' a 'special good mawnin' to you, Princess. Unfortunately, I haven't had the pleasure of acquaintance with this other young lady."

"This is my sister Roberta," Della said.

"It looks like we could use a doctor around here," the marshal said. "I'll send someone to round one up. There ought to be one around soon. About everybody this side of hell, beggin' your pardon, ladies, seems headin' this way. Mind if I ask a few questions, Princess?"

"You can stop calling me Princess," Della said. "My name is Della Judson, or did you know that?"

"Now, how would I know that?" the marshal returned. "I've met these other two gentlemen. Fact is, I've been trailin' Mr. Nello and his brothers for quite some time, along with these other officers with me. An' I tried to run Mr. Barret out of Gone Tomorrow before he got into trouble. Seems like he got into that trouble, after all. Was it you, Mr. Barret, who punctured Mr. Nello's leg with what, I take it, was a bullet? Do you want to tell me about it?"

"This ruffian was of a mind to kill Mr. Barret," Bobbie Judson spoke up pertly. "But he was a little slow. He should have known better. Mr. Barret is very fast. Very."

"So I've been told," Wheat said. "We've been trailin' the Nellos, for we had information they was mixed up in the stickup of a Santa Fe flyer a couple of months ago. And the information was right. We caught Art here, an'

173

Lige, who got himself killed, red-handed with the money. An' Mr. Barret here has shot the worst of the lot. Why?"

Again it was young Bobbie Judson who answered. "They acted like a bunch of claim jumpers, shooting up our house, taking a shot at Mr. Barret when he tried to talk sense to them."

"Claim?" Wheat said incredulously.

The two Pawnee trackers had been casting about. Vance saw them leaning from their horses, peering at the soil. He knew they had found the tracks of the blazeface horse, heading south out of the basin. They came, kicking their tired ponies into a shuffling trot, and whispered the news to Ben Wheat.

The marshal sighed and slid tiredly from his horse, which also drooped with weariness. "Now, that dugout looks like it might have been occupied for some time," he observed. "Some folks might say that you, Barret, an' Miss Judson soonered in. I'd think so myself if I didn't know better, bein' as I know that both of you was at the startin' line yesterday noon."

Again it was Bobbie who spoke. "We think buffalo hunters must have built the dugout in the old days when they poached down here in Indian hunting grounds. About the only way we stumbled on it was by luck."

"Or by knowin' about where to look for it," Wheat commented. "We caught a roan hawss up the country a piece. He looks like the roan the Princ—Miss Judson— was ridin' when the land run started."

He turned to Vance and asked blandly, "By the way, Mr. Barret, wasn't you ridin' that fast blazeface runner in the run? I don't see him around."

"Horses have a way of getting away from people," Vance said, equally bland.

Ben Wheat looked at his possemen. One,

authoritative of eye and bearing, smiled dryly and shrugged. "We've got the money, Ben," he said. "Wells Fargo is satisfied. You've got the Nellos. That'll satisfy Santa Fe."

It was over. The lawmen knew Frank Judson was riding for Texas on a horse that still had the strength to outdistance their mounts.

"Light down, gentlemen," Della said. "My sister and I better take a look at that gentleman's arm, as long as we're taking care of all the wounded. Then we'll fix up a bait of food. It doesn't look like your horses are in shape to head back north without considerable rest."

"Or south either," Ben Wheat said. "We'll accept your kind offer of hospitality for the night with grateful thanks."

It was a day later when Leatherwood, driving the lumbering medicine-show wagon, and Iggy, tooling the mules and the canvas-topped wagon, hove in sight. Henry Judson had recovered enough so that he was able to wave to his daughters from the wagon. Vance and the girls had been taking turns, watching the flats to the north until the wagons had appeared. It was Bobbie who had guided them into the basin.

Wheat and the posse had left a few hours earlier, taking Art Nello with them on horseback, and Chick Nello in an Army ambulance that they had managed to borrow. Ben Wheat had scoured around until he had rounded up seven settlers to serve on a coroner's jury, which returned a verdict that Lige Nello had been killed while resisting arrest. Vance had been told that Lige's body would occupy the first grave in cemetery land that had been set aside at a townsite which was springing up half a dozen miles east of their basin.

175

Leatherwood alighted from the wagon and gazed about, noting that claim stakes, flagged with scraps from petticoats and other feminine garb, waved in several directions in the basin. He stalked to the nearest and bent down, reading the inscription that had been scratched on the stake with a pocketknife. The claim, which included the dugout, the spring and the huge oak, was marked in the name of Vance Barret.

Leatherwood found claims fronting on the creek, and including stands of fine timber, staked out for him and Iggy. He returned to the wagons, where Vance and the girls had stood watching and waiting.

He glared belligerently at Vance. "Don't tell me you've gone loco. You ain't aimin' on bein' a sodbuster after all?"

"What's wrong with sodbusting?" Vance asked. "Maybe it's time you settled down too, you old wart hog, and raised turnips instead of hell."

Leatherwood looked more closely at Vance. Then at Della. She was smiling in that radiant, secret way of a woman who has found her full future.

"M'God!" Leatherwood groaned. "You two act like you was married."

"About three, four hours ago," Vance said. "I had a Wells Fargo agent fetch back a preacher as well as a doctor when he was looking for help. Ben Wheat was best man. We'll get the license as soon as the country gets organized."

Leatherwood uttered a pitiful groan. He watched Iggy let Bobbie lead him to where stakes bore the name of Ignacio G.Espinosa. Iggy wasn't paying much attention to what Bobbie was showing him. He was gazing, as though hypnotized, at her rich dark hair and supple figure. He kept stumbling over clods and clumps of grass

176

as he followed her around, taking every excuse to grasp her arm and assist her over obstacles that were not there.

Leatherwood uttered another groan of despair. "Me, what rode with Jubal Barret, with the Hole-in-the-Wall bunch, with the Robbers Roost boys, me that knew Hickok an' Earp an' Cody, me pitchin' hay to milk cows."

"You are about to start the best years of your life," Della said. "And the happiest."

We hope that you enjoyed reading this
Sagebrush Large Print Western.
If you would like to read more Sagebrush titles,
ask your librarian or contact the Publishers:

United States and Canada

Thomas T. Beeler, *Publisher*
Post Office Box 659
Hampton Falls, New Hampshire 03844-0659
(800) 251-8726

United Kingdom, Eire, and
the Republic of South Africa

Isis Publishing Ltd
7 Centremead
Osney Mead
Oxford OX2 0ES England
(01865) 250333

Australia and New Zealand

Australian Large Print Audio & Video P/L
17 Mohr Street
Tullamarine, Victoria, 3043, Australia
1 800 335 364